Sue's Fingerprint

Andrew D. Carlson

SUE'S FINGERPRINT

ISBN: 0-615-45622-7
ISBN-13: 978-0-615-45622-5

Dedication

To David

Acknowledgement

Thanks to my family for allowing me to embark on a second career, and for having patience with me along the way.

Prologue

The scientist walked to the building entrance and opened the door for his guest. "Thank you for visiting, sir. We appreciate you taking the time. I certainly understand your interest in this."

The two men walked down the hall to the laboratory. The scientist unlocked the door with his key card and held it open for his guest. As they walked to the lab bench, he said, "If you see in this box here…"

The guest peered over the edge of the box.

"Oh, don't worry, sir. It's Plexiglas. Nothing will happen. It can't get out. Now, if we take a normal lab mouse, like this, and place it in the box… Watch how it moves… And look! Now we have *two* mice! I don't know what this is, sir, but it sure isn't from this planet."

Chapter 1 – Not Normal

Karen heard *pop pop pop* as she sat on her bed reading her Fifty State Shapes book. She looked out the window for the source of the noise but saw only her swing set and her mother's garden. She returned to reading her book.

"Sweetie, I have to go down the street to Mrs. Clark's house," her mother called from the kitchen. "I promised to drop off some tomatoes. I'll be right back. Don't go anywhere and don't answer the phone, okay?"

"Okay mommy. I'll be good. I'll just read in my room."

"I'll only be gone for fifteen minutes or so. Bye sweetie."

"Bye mommy!"

Above the background swoosh of the summer breeze rustling the tree leaves outside, Karen became aware of a scratching noise. She looked at her gerbil cage and smiled, comforted by the sight of Patches.

She resumed her reading, but again she heard scratching. It was louder, and it wasn't Patches. Karen glanced out the window and saw a ground squirrel come into view. It scratched around the edge of the grass where it met the mulch a couple feet from the window in the back of the split-level house.

"Hello there," she said with a smile. "What's your name?

1

My name is Karen. You're cute! Whatchya doing?" She watched the animal scratching with purpose in the mulch, inching closer. "You're a furry little guy. What do you smell over there?"

As she talked, the rodent made its way across the mulch toward the screen of her open window. "You're not scared of me, are you?"

Karen kneeled on her bed at the window and slid the screen open to get a closer look at the rodent. The squirrel quickly hopped toward the open window. "Whoa! You can't come in here!"

She slid the screen closed as fast as she could, but the squirrel didn't run away. It backed up a bit and continued to scratch in the mulch, waiting for another opportunity.

Karen's face went from smile to scowl. She didn't like the way the squirrel was behaving. *It almost jumped in my room!*

She hopped off her bed, found the small broom in the laundry room, and brought it back to her bedroom. She slid open the screen and jabbed at the squirrel to knock it away. And she actually hit it. *But why didn't it run away?*

Dazed, the squirrel slowly got back on its feet and returned to the same spot by the window. Karen closed the screen. She was confused. It should have run when she hit it. She opened the screen again to knock the rodent away a second time. It tumbled again, but did not run away. She frowned at the squirrel. *He's not normal.*

Suddenly, the squirrel jumped to its feet and hopped toward the open window.

"Oh, no you don't!" Karen yelled as she closed the window screen. "You're not coming in my room! Go away! Shoo!"

Hearing the shout, the squirrel finally ran away. Karen did not take her eyes off the rodent as it scurried away.

Down the road and across the street from Karen's house

lived a mystery man. His neighbors frequently saw him maintaining his house or his truck, or going to and from… no one really knew. David was not well known around town.

He was a little taller than most but didn't stand out in a crowd. He wasn't very old, mid-forties, but he looked older than he actually was. He was scruffy and rugged. Clearly, he was a former military man. He retained his good physique, continued to cut his hair short, and wore his Swiss Army military watch at all times.

In the afternoon sun, David emerged from his garage carrying a BB gun. He walked in front of his truck, which was not, nor ever, parked in the garage, and headed around the side of the house to the backyard. His backyard could have been a small farm or a grassy prairie. Instead, the yard served as two acres of prime burrowing real-estate.

"Damn gophers."

As he continued out into the yard with his gun, he surveyed the number of burrow holes in the yard. He slowed his pace and eventually stopped walking. His eyebrows rose. The scowl on his face turned confusion. "Did I have this many last year?" he asked himself. "Something's not right. There are *way* too many holes out here."

An afternoon sporting event became a chore, but was still a challenge. David walked to the side of the house, turned on the water spigot and dragged the hose out into the yard. He started filling holes. After a minute or two of waiting, a gopher emerged. David fired his gun. "Ha! Take that Mr. Gopher!"

Feeling quite pleased, David repositioned his hose into another nearby hole and waited again. After a moment passed, "Yes! Another one bites the dust!"

David repositioned his hose again. "What the…? This is too easy. They keep coming out. Gophers aren't normally that stupid."

He repositioned his hose yet again. After another

moment, "What the hell is going on?"

He didn't fire his gun, but waited, with the water still flooding his yard. Another gopher popped out of the ground, followed by another. David was stunned. He could only wonder what was happening under his yard. *If they're coming up this quickly with just water, there must be a ton of 'em under there. How many, and why are they so dumb?*

He quickly shot the gophers that came up to the surface and weren't smart enough to find an un-flooded hole to crawl down. Then he dragged the hose to the side of the house and turned off the water. He went into the garage and emerged with a determined look on his face, riding his lawn tractor fitted with his snow-thrower attachment. He was on a mission.

David rode out to the far end of his lot. He engaged the snow-thrower and moved from one side of the lot to the other, in parallel rows toward the house, throwing dirt and gopher bits to the side of the tractor.

When he reached the patio, David drove his muddy tractor around the side of the house to the hose. He grumbled to himself as he rinsed off the snow-thrower. Several obscenities and utterances of the word "gopher" filled the air. He was both annoyed and confused.

Chapter 2 - Goo

Dr. James Bailey drove to his lab, Manhattan Laboratory Services, located in an unmarked building in an industrial park in Manhattan, Kansas. He was late.

He had been Director of the laboratory for three years, but had worked there much longer. The lab had seen good times; testing potential anthrax letters for authenticity was, for his lab, good business. And they had struggled through slow times, when few security events required his lab's attention. Usually, his government contract laboratory tested prisoners' DNA samples for future criminal investigations. But a few weeks earlier, to his excitement, the lab had been selected for a "special project."

Carrying a pile of loosely-stacked papers in his arms and his computer bag slung over his shoulder, he walked from his car across the parking lot to the entrance. Jim was of average height and average build. Well, maybe the years caught up to him a little around the middle. As usual, he wore casual slacks, a button-up shirt, and a sport coat.

Jim entered the building and walked past the labs, straight to the small meeting room in the back of the building. "Sorry I'm late," he apologized as he walked in the room.

Two of the lab's group leaders, Cindy Gordon and Sarah

Deming, were waiting for him. Cindy was lanky and tough. Sarah was feisty and boisterous. Both were very smart. And both were happy to be working at MLS. The loved the science and the secret nature of their business, and were glad it was a job at which they could wear jeans and t-shirts under their white lab coats.

"Thanks for being here so early. I know you're busy." Jim took a seat and started the meeting. "Someone from Homeland Security is coming in two days to get an initial briefing. We have to have our presentation ready. So let's get to it." Looking through his papers, he started to review events. "Let's start from the... er... beginning," he suggested. "Two weeks ago, a sheriff in... Where was that?"

"Duncan, Oklahoma," Cindy responded.

"Right, Oklahoma. He found a two-inch puddle of slime on the hood of his patrol car. It was steaming and smelled. Being the rather paranoid person that he was, he called his local contact in Homeland Security."

"Correct," confirmed Cindy.

"And when we got there, we scraped it off the car with a plastic spatula and placed it in a sample tube, right?"

"Yes."

"What did we do with it when we got it back here?" Jim asked.

"I had my group split up the sample and started to analyze it," explained Cindy. "We started with pretty simple physical tests. Then we had to get more complicated to figure out what it was."

"And basically the slime is comprised of phospholipid bilayers."

"Yep, it is, with really big membrane proteins that we couldn't identify. Under the microscope it basically looks like empty cells with huge proteins. But this stuff is weird. I've never seen anything quite like it."

"So then we got a call from a rancher in New Mexico, correct?" Jim asked. "He found some next to his animal's water trough and called his county sheriff who called DHS who called us, right?"

"Yep," Cindy replied.

"And the analysis of those samples?"

"Same thing. We think the proteins may be receptors to move stuff into the cells, but we haven't been able to figure out what they're specific for."

"Since then we've had calls from a guy who owns a ski lodge in Colorado," Jim added. "Frozen blobs of goo were found on the tables of his outdoor deck. Can you believe it's snowing up in the mountains already?" he asked. "And the department got a call from a lady in Iowa who almost slipped on the stuff as she was cleaning out her garage. Same goo, right?"

"Not quite," Sarah interjected. "Remember, that's when we had our little anomaly. We tested the stuff on the mice to see if it irritated the skin or got any kind of reaction. I started with the Colorado goo. We put some on one of the mice. Nothing happened. Then we mixed some with water and it foamed up like soap. We gave another mouse a nice shampoo," she laughed. "Then we took the Iowa goo and put it on a third mouse. Nothing... or so we thought. I got a towel to wipe the stuff off the three mice and--"

"There were four mice," Jim replied.

"There were four mice," Sarah confirmed.

"So now it gets complicated," Jim continued. "Did you repeat your experiment on another mouse?"

"Yes, but all we had left was some of the Colorado goo. Nothing happened."

"Then we got a new sample yesterday, from Kansas City, correct?"

"Yes," Cindy said. "A big blob of the stuff was found on the side of a fire station, in the shadow of the building. The crew returned from a call and was putting the trucks away. The chief noticed it and called his police buddies who called DHS who called us."

"And?"

"We collected the sample," Cindy said. "Actually, there was quite a lot... like, twice as much as usual. We ran our basic tests. It's the same stuff as the other goo."

Sarah added, "I gave some to Helen this morning for another animal experiment."

With perfect timing, Helen entered the room. Her face was pale. She was followed by a gaggle of technicians, including a younger tech named Scott, each as stunned as Helen. "It did it again!" Helen gasped. "One minute, one mouse, the next minute... *two* mice!"

"It was totally psycho," added Scott. "We put the mouse in an empty cage with the goo. The mouse went and sniffed at it... stuck its nose in the stuff. And then, like, the stuff oozed and swelled up, and right before our eyes... another mouse. This is totally jacked up, man."

They all sat for a few moments, trying to digest the news. What was it that happened? Two times it had occurred. Both times: two mice from one mouse.

The silence was broken by Jim. "Can I put that in my report, Scott? The results are 'totally jacked up'."

Everyone laughed.

Looking to Sarah, Jim asked, "Can we repeat these 'results' again?"

"Do we have any of the Kansas City goo left, Helen?" Sarah asked. "That seems to be good goo. The Colorado goo wasn't good."

"Yeah, I saved some," Helen responded. "I hope it's stable."

"We'll have to assume it is," Jim said.

Chapter 3 - Go Find Out

Ted Stevens sat at his desk, clicking through email messages and scanning departmental memos. The work in front of him didn't interest Ted in the least. He wanted to get out in the field.

Ted was a government man for life. After getting a college degree in chemistry, he's worked for nearly thirty years as an aide, an assistant, an agent, a lackey, a minion, and every other position in the various offices that have been lumped under the DHS. He eventually worked his way up the chain of command to reach the position of Director for the Chemical and Biological Division within the DHS Science and Technology Directorate. His business card simply read: "Director, DHS."

His title gave him the authority to direct the activities of those that reported to him, as well as those with whom DHS had contracts. Interacting with the people on the outside, the scientists and analysts, was what Ted liked best. He hated sitting in his office in Washington, DC. Mindlessly shuffling papers nearly put him to sleep.

Thankfully, his boredom was interrupted. The directorate's Chief of Staff charged into Ted's office. "Stevens!"

"Um… Hello, sir. To what do I owe the honor?"

"We have a new assignment for you."

Ted sat up in his chair, listening closely.

"We've identified a possible new threat that we want you, not one of your people, to investigate. You see, a sticky, gel-like material has been reported at various locations. Local law enforcement agencies have called it in."

"Sticky, gel-like material?"

"Correct. One of our labs, in Kansas, has been dispatched to collect samples of the stuff and analyze it. They've started their investigation. You're point on this one, Ted. Go find out what this is all about."

"Why me? Someone found some slime out there and you're sending a *director* to find out what it is? This assignment is at least two pay grades below me."

The chief of staff shrugged in response.

"Don't get me wrong," Ted added, "I don't mind getting out of this office, but don't you think a junior staffer can take this?"

"All I know is the Secretary said it had to be a director."

"This has gone all the way to the top?" Ted asked. "The Secretary's involved?"

"Yes."

"Okay," Ted replied with a nod. "I can't refuse an assignment. I'll go look at the stuff."

"Use whatever resources you need," the chief told him. "A jet is at your disposal."

"Thanks. I guess I'll go pack for a trip to Kansas."

Chapter 4 - Goldilocks

"Okay, Mr. Stevens arrives tomorrow," Jim told his group leaders. "Should I summarize what we know?"

Sarah and Cindy nodded.

"The goo..." He stopped and shook his head. "We have got to find a better term for this stuff... but I guess we'll worry about that later," he said waving his hand. "The goo that's been collected appears to be empty cells. There are a few large membrane proteins in the lipid bilayer of the cells, but no internal cellular structures. Correct?"

"That's what it looks like," Cindy replied. "And I actually did a lot of searching on the internet yesterday, but I couldn't find any explanation for this stuff anywhere. It's like it fell out the sky from outer space or something. It's weird."

"Weird is right," Jim concurred. "When you rub the Colorado goo on a mouse, it gets clean. But when you rub the Iowa or Kansas City goo on a mouse, another one appears from out of the goo."

"Uh... yeah," Sarah responded. "But it sounds kinda stupid when you say it like that."

Cindy corrected her, "I believe you mean 'jacked up'."

They all laughed.

"So let's think about this and come up with some possible explanations," Jim suggested.

"There are none," Sarah said. "This is beyond explainable."

"Can we try? We have to at least attempt to provide an explanation for Mr. Stevens. Now, we know the stuff is basically empty cells with huge membrane proteins. But it's not something anyone has seen before. And when it contacts a mouse, another mouse is created from the goo." He paused to let the summary sink in.

"Assuming normal biology and chemistry is at play... Okay, never mind," he said. "Let's assume *anything* is possible. Could the substance use DNA to transform into an animal?"

"Yeah, I guess. The cellular proteins could be DNA receptors," Cindy said.

"How likely is it that they are DNA receptors?"

"I have no idea," Cindy replied.

"Do either of you have any other thoughts what they might be?"

Neither Cindy nor Sarah had another suggestion.

"Well... it's our best guess right now. Let's assume they're DNA receptors," Jim said. "So the receptors come in contact with animal DNA and turn on some sort of metamorphosis. The cells take the form of the animal from which the DNA came. The goo clones the animal."

"This stuff is not from this planet," Sarah said.

"But the goo only responds to DNA when it... what?" asked Jim. "What was different between the Oklahoma, New Mexico, Colorado, Iowa, and Kansas City goo?"

"Time," Cindy suggested. "The active goo was collected recently."

"Fresh goo versus old goo?" Jim asked.

"What about heat? Could that have degraded the goo?" Sarah proposed.

"It might have fried the goo from the hood of the car in Oklahoma or the New Mexico ranch, but the Colorado goo didn't transform into a mouse and it was cold there," Cindy said.

"But it was frozen," Jim noted. "Freezing might also degrade it."

"We found the Kansas City goo in the shade and it was active," added Sarah. "Where was the Iowa stuff found?"

"In an old lady's garage," Cindy responded. "It was in the shade and it was active."

"Not too hot, not too cold."

"So temperature extremes may degrade the goo. If it's not just right where the goo is, it can't transform," Jim summarized.

"Goldilocks goo," Sarah said.

"Interesting," Jim responded.

He and the group leaders began to write up the information for the next day's presentation. They documented the history of the samples they collected. They documented the analyses they conducted. They struggled to make a plausible explanation for the nature of the goo and the transformations of the mice, but science couldn't explain it… at least not science here on Earth.

At the end of the day, they put the finishing touches on their presentation and hoped that Mr. Stevens, a government man, would be able to follow along.

Scott walked into the meeting room. "Hey, what if a person touches this stuff?"

ANDREW D. CARLSON

Chapter 5 - What Would Happen

Dr. Jim Bailey couldn't sleep. He laid awake thinking.

What would happen if the goo came in contact with human DNA? That is not an experiment my lab is going to conduct. I've got to remember to institute full protection procedures. We cannot allow that to happen.

As he rolled over in bed, trying to get comfortable, he reflected on his past. When he received his Ph.D. in Biochemistry, he certainly didn't expect to be investigating alien goo. He liked his current position; he enjoyed conducting science in relative anonymity. And he liked the people that worked for him. But sometimes the "projects" were a little strange.

His thoughts returned to the next day's meeting. He wasn't sure what Mr. Stevens would say when he received the briefing.

What will he think? Will he understand the nature of the goo? And where is the goo coming from? Outer space? Really? And did we collect all of it? Surely not. There has to be more out there that people haven't found yet. But what has become of that goo?

Jim knew this was only the beginning.

Chapter 6 – Show Time

As he drove from the airport, Ted Stevens called ahead to notify the director, a Dr. Bailey, that he would arrive shortly.

After hanging up the phone, he rubbed his head and wondered just where these new findings would eventually lead him.

How many times in the past twenty-seven years have I been forced to chase ghosts? Too many times to count. But who knows? This time might be different.

The official mission of Ted's division was to increase the nation's awareness and preparedness against chemical and biological threats through advanced surveillance, detection, and protective countermeasures. Today, his mission was to get a briefing from the contract laboratory in Manhattan, Kansas.

He leaned back in his seat and tried to relax.

The lab results might be significant. This 'gel-like material' might really be a new threat. Or maybe I'm chasing snot.

But no... From the number of reports we've received, it's significant. When we get just one call to the office, it's always a hoax. Two calls are a coincidence. Three calls are a trend. With as many as we've received, we should be concerned. But what could it be?

Jim went straight to the front conference room, the one used for visitors. It was the only room with windows. He called Cindy and Sarah to join him from the lab. After a few minutes spent setting up the presentation and getting coffee, the three scientists sat in the conference room waiting for Mr. Stevens to arrive. They sat in silence. No one really wanted to re-visit yesterday's discussions any sooner than they had to.

Five minutes later, a black sedan pulled into the parking lot. An average-sized, aging man with grey hair climbed out of the car. He wore a black suit, and carried a black portfolio.

"Show time," Jim announced as he saw his guest walk to the entrance. He stood and left the conference room. He walked to the front door and opened it for his guest. "Good morning Mr. Stevens. My name is James Bailey. I'm the Director here at the lab."

"Good morning. Please, call me Ted."

Dr. Bailey led the way. "Here we are, in this conference room. Can I get you anything... coffee, soda?"

"No, thank you. I'm good to go."

Jim introduced Cindy and Sarah, and they all took their seats. "Thank you for visiting, sir," Jim said. "We appreciate you taking the time. I can certainly understand your interest in this."

"Ha! 'Interest' is putting it mildly," Ted replied.

"Shall we begin?" Jim asked. "Please, stop us at any time if you have questions."

Ted motioned for him to begin.

Dr. Bailey began the presentation with the time table of events, starting with the first discovery of the goo in Oklahoma.

Mr. Stevens made notes on the locations and dates of the discoveries. The questions he asked indicated that he understood the physical state of the substance. But as they got deeper into the biochemistry, Ted looked to be in over his head. His attention faded when the topic of animal transformation was discussed. After hearing the details about the two-mice experiment, Ted simply stared out the window.

Jim waited for Ted to respond. He waited for several moments.

"Oh, sorry," Ted finally apologized, snapping to attention after he detected the prolonged silence in the room. "I checked out there for a while, didn't I?" He chuckled at himself, but then his grin slowly faded. "The idea of duplicate animals, clones, got me thinking about the possible effects out there," he said, pointing out the windows. "This could get ugly."

Jim made him an offer. "Mr. Stevens, would you like to go into the lab and see the substance?"

"Yes, I think I need to go see this stuff. Is it safe?"

"Yes sir, nothing to worry about. Please, follow me."

They left the conference room and walked down the hall to the lab. Jim unlocked the door with his key card and held it open for Ted, Cindy, and Sarah. "Please put on a lab coat and safety goggles," Jim instructed, "laboratory regulations, you know. But don't worry, you won't need the protection as long as you don't touch anything.

"Over here sir… you can see how we found it," Jim said as they walked to the lab bench. "Doesn't look like much of anything, eh? But we managed to do some interesting experiments. We've achieved amazing results. Let me show you. If you see in this box here…"

Ted hesitantly peered over the edge of the box, not knowing what to expect.

"Oh, don't worry. It's Plexiglas. Nothing will happen. It can't get out. Now… if we take a normal lab mouse like this, and place it in the box… Watch how it moves… And look! Once we had a blob of substance, and now we have two mice!"

Ted could only stare in amazement at what he just saw.

"It's some sort of weird mutation," Jim quietly told himself. "It starts out amorphous, with no speciation… then it comes in contact with an animal and… wow." He turned to Ted with a nervous look. "I don't know what this is, but it sure isn't from this planet."

"So," Ted began, straight-faced, "let me see if I can summarize. The substance that is appearing all over the country, from Iowa to New Mexico, is alien goo. And it has huge proteins in it which DNA fits, like a key. And when unlocked, the goo turns into animals. Did I get that correct?"

"Simply speaking, yes," Jim confirmed.

"Or rather…" Ted added with a sly grin, "when the membrane-bound receptors in the phospholipid bilayer bind to DNA from a donor animal, the substance is stimulated to transform, cloning the donor animal." He looked at Jim and smiled.

Jim was wide-eyed with surprise.

"You didn't think I could understand it all, did you?" Ted asked him.

"Er…"

Ted lost his smile, cocked his head, and rubbed his chin. "So tell me," he said, "if it's not from this planet, where is it from?"

"Um…"

"And what if the donor animal is a human?"

"I don't know, sir."

Chapter 7 – The Smartest

"How do you like your new teacher this week?" Karen's mother asked, as she moved between the sink, counter and stove, preparing dinner. "Is she still as nice as you thought last week?"

"Well, she might have slipped to a nine," Karen replied. She sat on a chair at the kitchen table, doodling on a piece of paper. "But, she might still be a ten. She got mad at Colt in class today. He was just talking to Allison. He wasn't doing anything bad, but Mrs. Ryan kinda yelled at him. I felt bad for him. He didn't look sad, but I think he was. He's a nice boy. So I'll have to see how Mrs. Ryan is tomorrow before I can officially lower her to a nine. But she still likes me and doesn't get mad at me, so she's still really nice."

"She's not an eight then?"

"No way. She's definitely at least a nine, but not Mr. Butterfield. He's the janitor. He's mean. We all call him Mr. Butterbutt," Karen said proudly with a smile on her face.

"I'm sorry to hear that he's mean."

"He tries to sweep the floor but kids get in his way. He gets madder. That makes him meaner."

"Do you think he's mean because all the kids try to be mean to him?"

After reflection, Karen replied, "Maybe… but you can't be mean to kids no matter what they do to you."

Karen had medium-length blonde hair and blue eyes. She was tall for her age, active, and fit. She loved to be outside. But she also enjoyed reading books. And she liked to watch TV, when her mother let her.

"So did anything else happen at school today?" her mother asked. "Anything good?" she clarified.

"Ricky was gluing the holiday pieces on his calendar and he took the glue stick and put it on his lips like lipstick. He left it there and then his lips stuck!" She laughed. "They didn't get totally stuck, just a little stuck. It was so funny!"

"Sweetie, are you adjusting well in class? You're younger than the other kids. They're all seven, while you're a year younger."

"I like the other kids, Mommy. And I'm not too young. I'm not the only one who's six. Of all the kids, I think I'm the smartest." She smiled.

Karen and her mother enjoyed their conversations in the kitchen each evening before dinner. Talking kept them close, which was important, since it was just the two of them in the house.

Changing the subject, her mother asked, "Did you see Mrs. Clark's new car? It's really small, isn't it?"

"Yeah," Karen replied. "Why?"

"She wants to use less gas when she drives. She's being green."

"Why is the backyard of the man over there all muddy?" Karen asked, pointing across the street towards David's house. "He's being brown, not green."

"I don't know, dear. A few days ago it was grass, now its mud."

"What's his name?"

"David, I think," her mother replied.

"David."

After a moment of silence spent looking out over the garden in the back yard, her mother started another subject.

"Do you think the pumpkins in the garden will be big enough this year for carving jack-o-lanterns?"

"Yeah! I want to carve one this year, okay mommy?"

"I think so, with my help."

"Remember the ones you carved last year? You made an Elmo pumpkin!"

"And a Cookie Monster," her mother added.

"They were really funny. But I don't like Sesame Street anymore. I like Phineas and Ferb. They build cool stuff and do funny things."

"Is that what you're watching at free time now?" her mother asked. "What about Dora the Explorer?"

"Boring! Nope. I like Phineas and Ferb. And Perry. He's their platypus."

"Platypus? Okay..." her mother said, shaking her head. "Dinner's ready. Are you?"

"Yup!"

"Please wash your hands."

"Okay."

Chapter 8 - A Pod

Collecting alien goo had become routine and uneventful. When lab techs were called out to recover blobs of goo, they mostly found unstable goo that could not do its special trick. So Bruno Jones did not have high expectations when the team left the lab for his recovery one morning.

Bruno nicely complimented the other two group leaders at Manhattan Laboratory Services. He, too, lived for science, having received a Ph.D. And he enjoyed the added bonus of being able to wear jeans and a t-shirt at work. He wasn't a suit and tie guy, not even a button-up shirt guy.

When Bruno and the team arrived at the entrance to a municipal park near the lab in Manhattan, they surveyed the scene. Near the hedges that border the park gate, they found the blob of goo, right where the police had said it was. They recorded the location, described the condition of the goo, and transferred it to the collection tubes with the usual care.

Bruno inspected the area within two or three feet of the blob to make sure they had not overlooked anything. Under a nearby shrub, he made perhaps the most important discovery since the goo itself. Bruno Jones found a pod.

Excited about a potential breakthrough in the investigation, Bruno crawled under the shrub to get a close look. He described the new find to one of the lab technicians, who took notes. "It's a clear plastic sphere, about the size of a ping pong ball. It looks like a paintball, except bigger, with no color. There is a hole in the top, like it was carved out."

He carefully examined the top of the sphere without touching it and continued dictating to the technician. "It looks like it's filled with goo. Or maybe water... I can't tell. The ground is wet where we found the blob of substance. But it's not really wet under this shrub where the pod is."

Bruno crawled out from under the shrub. He looked around at the surrounding bushes and grass. He continued making observations, mostly to himself. He wasn't concerned about the lab tech taking notes. He was too occupied by the scene. "The sprinkler system was recently turned on. The blob is on the wet ground close to the grass. The pod, though, is further back under the shrub. The water was not sprayed under the shrub, so the water under the shrub would have dropped off the leaves. That's why the ground isn't very wet near the pod."

He thought about the situation for a moment to find an explanation. Suddenly, he had an epiphany. "That's why the pod has a hole in the top! A drop of water landed on it from the shrub above! It dissolved the pod! Like acid eating a hole in it! The goo near the grass was a blob because the pod that contained it dissolved in the water from the sprinklers! Water! Water dissolves the pods that carry the goo!"

Bruno asked for the recovery log and began to record his own notes. It took him several minutes to write down all of his observations.

With double-gloved hands, he carefully picked up the pod and looked inside the top. He assumed the goo was still in the pod. He angled a sample tube and placed his fingers that held the pod as far inside as possible. He slowly released the pod, hoping to not damage it or the goo inside. He would have to wait until he got back to the lab to see how successful he was.

Bruno unloaded the van and quickly entered the lab.

Sarah happened to meet Bruno in the hallway and greeted him. "Doctor Jones! Wha'sup?"

"I found it! I found a pod!"

"A what?" she asked.

"A pod! The vessel the goo comes in! We found one!" Bruno said as he continued walking down the hall. "It was next to a normal sample. You know... a blob. It's in a tube. We put the pod in a tube! We have it! We have to test it to see if the stuff inside really is goo. Let's go!"

Sarah didn't bother to ask for clarification. She followed Bruno into the animal lab and set up the normal experiment. She got the Plexiglas box and a mouse, and waited for Bruno to give her the sample.

Cindy had overheard the excitement when Bruno returned. She joined the others in the lab, along with Dr. Bailey.

Bruno placed the small cooler containing the samples onto the lab bench. He opened the cooler, removed the blob sample, and tossed it aside with a been-there-done-that attitude. He carefully removed the tube containing the pod. All eyes were on him and the sample. He opened the tube and carefully used a lab spatula to extract the pod. It spun a couple times; everyone gasped and held their breath, but the substance inside didn't leak out. He set the pod in a plastic petri dish.

"Now what?" Bruno asked. "Do we cut it open? Squeeze the stuff out? Place it into the box just like it is?"

"I don't think we want to cut it," Jim suggested. "That may damage or contaminate it."

"The other samples have moved... oozed... when they came in contact with the mouse. Can it ooze out of the pod?" asked Sarah.

"Maybe gently squeezing the goo out is the best," Cindy recommended. "That shouldn't damage it. We've recovered stable samples that have been through worse. And then it would be free of the pod with, you know… room to grow."

"I like Cindy's idea," Jim said. "Let's carefully squeeze the stuff out into the box, but only squeeze out about half. Keep the rest for analysis. And keep the pod. We need to study it too."

Bruno double-gloved his hand and carefully picked up the pod. He placed it in the Plexiglas box, inverted the pod and squeezed half the contents out through the hole. "The pod is pretty flexible," he informed the others.

Everyone crowded around the box to observe. The mouse came over to sniff the substance. Within a few seconds after touching the substance, same as with stable samples previously-tested, the mouse was joined by a second.

The lab had the proof they needed. The goo was originally contained in clear, flexible, gelatin-like, ping pong ball-sized pods.

Bruno placed the half-squeezed pod back in the petri dish. He and Cindy started to plan the experiments they could run to analyze the rest of the goo and the composition of the pod. Others talked about how they would have to change the recovery protocols to look for pods.

Jim stood in the middle of the lab while the others scurried around him. His mind was spinning. *This has to be how the substance was delivered to Earth. But it couldn't have been sent to Earth in the pod. Or could it? Could the pod survive the extreme radiation, near absolute-zero temperatures, and the vacuum of space? How could it not burn up upon entry through the atmosphere? How could it not explode upon impact, splattering goo several feet? Was the pod protected? How? Who sent the pods? From where?*

Many unanswered questions remained.

Chapter 9 - The Strangest Thing

David decided that a week was enough time to wait before surveying the state of his backyard. The damage he did should have healed so that driving over the ground was possible.

He drove his lawn tractor out of the garage and headed out back. As he began his drive over the dry, tilled ground, he noticed the remains of several animals and almost no sign of fresh burrowing. Had his strategy worked? Had he eliminated the gophers? Feeling good with himself, he sat up a bit higher and continued to drive.

But pride soon turned to confusion. As he approached the far end of his lot, he noticed gophers. They weren't alive. But they were intact.

He stopped his tractor and got off. He walked among the dozen carcasses, doing his best impersonation of a crime scene investigation. The gophers were not all that close to each other. They were lying on top of the tilled soil, all facing towards the house--the only structure in the near vicinity. They seemed to have been there for a day or two. Their fur was dry, crusty, and bleached. There was no injury to any of the bodies, as far as he could see. He lightly kicked a few to flip them over for a different view.

Realizing he didn't have the training required to further investigate, David drove back to the garage to get a trash bag and shovel. He returned to the end of the lot and bagged the dead animals.

When he pulled into the garage with his bag of gophers, David received a visitor: Deputy Sheriff Bill Leland, also known around town as Spike.

Deputy Leland got his nickname from his spiked crew-cut hair. He was young, tall, and muscular. He looked intimidating, but folks who knew him liked him. Spike took the time to chat with as many people in the county as he could, as often as he could. He liked to know what was going on. Sharing information, he thought, deterred criminals and prevented crime.

Spike pulled up and got out of his cruiser. "Afternoon, David."

"Spike, how are you? What brings you out here?"

"Rumor in town is you went loco and dug up your yard. I see it's true. What gives?"

"I got sick of mowing."

"No, really David, why'd you till it up?"

"Gophers."

"Gophers?

"Had a bumper crop and couldn't store 'em all for the winter. So I had to till 'em under."

Spike rolled his eyes. He had been around enough to know when he was not getting a straight answer. But he didn't lose his composure; he needed to talk to David. "Anyone else around here have gopher problems?"

"Don't think so," David replied.

"I haven't heard of others in the area having the same problem... just you."

"What are you getting at, Spike?"

"I don't know," he said, scratching his head. "It seems odd that only one piece of land would have a gopher problem while every other acre in the county is normal."

David looked into Spike's eyes and realized he was not

just poking around to get the latest dirt to support local gossip. He knew Spike wanted to understand why the gopher infestation only occurred in his yard. He decided to soften up and help. "You want the scoop?"

"Please."

"A little over a week ago, I started to notice gopher holes in the yard," David began. "And then more and still more. They just kept appearing. I knew I had to do something. I didn't think it was bad enough for harsh chemicals, so I decided to have a little fun with my BB gun. I flooded a few tunnels and picked a few off." He chuckled, mainly to himself, and then changed his expression. "But there were more out there than I expected... a lot more. I stopped screwin' around and got out the tractor. I don't grow anything, so I didn't have a tiller. But," he said with a grin, "the snow thrower worked."

Spike laughed.

"Funny thing was, though, now that I think about it, I actually killed gophers. They aren't that stupid, are they? They normally burrow when they get scared. Wouldn't you think they would have gone deep?"

"You would've thought," Spike replied.

"I was just out there and found the strangest thing. Most of the gophers were gone... you know, no longer in one piece, except for a few that were lying dead on the dirt, out of the tunnels. They've been dead for a day or two. They were all facing the same direction, towards the house. I wonder what that means. Anyways, I got 'em here in the bag."

"Hmm... that's interesting." Spike paused to think, and then looked David in the eyes and asked, "Can you keep a secret?" He didn't wait for David to respond before continuing. "The DHS network has had reports of strange stuff goin' on. Not the false terror alarms... those are always fake," he said with a brush of his hand. "These are reports of some pretty strange stuff, like goop being found here and there, more rats than usual, raccoons being more aggressive to get inside barns and shelters... even in broad daylight. I wonder if your gophers are related."

David stood there with his mouth open in disbelief. Was Spike feeding him a load of crap, or was he serious? *DHS network? Goop? Aggressive raccoons?*

"What are you doing with those?" Spike asked.

"The dead gophers? Nothing," David replied. "You want 'em? Take 'em."

He gave the bag to Spike who took it to the car and put it in the trunk. With a serious look, Spike made a last request of David. "Please keep this quiet. I need to ask around the network to see if your gophers are tied into this in any way. I'll let you know what I find out. I promise. But let's keep this between us for now."

"Uh... yeah, you bet... just between us," David said, looking hesitantly at Spike. "See ya."

Deputy Leland got in his cruiser and waved to David as he drove out.

David stood in his driveway for a few minutes. If anyone had been watching they'd have thought he was frozen in place. He tried to understand the events of the past hour, from rounding up dead gophers to "goop" on the "network". He eventually snapped out of his trance, put his tractor away, and went inside for a beer.

Chapter 10 - An Outbreak

Jim, Cindy, Sarah, and Bruno assembled in the front conference room. They were all tired. They worked late the day before to review the events of the past week, compile the available data, and complete the presentation for Mr. Stevens. All four made sure they had enough coffee for the meeting.

A black sedan pulled into the parking lot. A man in a black suit emerged, carrying his black portfolio.

Dr. Bailey met him at the front door. "Good morning, sir."

"Arr."

"I hope you'll explain what that means," Jim told his guest.

The two men entered the conference room and everyone took their seats. Mr. Stevens kicked off the meeting. It was clear he was burdened with something. "I want to give you all some information before you update me on what you've found." He paused for a moment or two, and then continued. "Many zoos are reporting more animals."

The lab employees looked at each other, confused.

Ted clarified, "More monkeys, lemurs... primates... in their habitats... you know, cages. There are usually a lot of these animals in the cages, so no visitor has noticed. Word of the extra animals hasn't leaked yet, as far as we know. But one zoo reported a new bear cub that appeared one day. That's something you can't simply hope no one will notice. The mother and her... now *two* cubs were 'temporarily moved inside for better care from the zoo staff'. And the weird thing is some of the zoos are reporting more deaths of animals. Not many at each zoo, but from the reports we're receiving, it seems to be a trend. There are more instances of deaths in the African-savannah type exhibits than in the tropical exhibits... jungles. Do you have any data to help explain?"

"More animals than they're supposed to have?" Jim asked for clarification, "and a higher incidence of deaths in the hot, arid exhibits?"

"Yes."

Sarah commented, "If we're finding stable goo that can transform mice here in the lab, it's likely the goo is transforming into more animals out in the wild."

They all gave the idea some thought.

"What happened with your mice here in the lab is happening out there on a grand scale?" Ted confirmed.

"It's likely," Jim replied.

"An outbreak of alien transformations," Bruno added.

Ted thought more about that idea. "This cannot be good," he said. He shook his head and sat for a moment. Then he changed the subject. "New data?" he asked. "Do you have new data for me?"

Cindy sat up in her chair. She began downloading information to Mr. Stevens. "We've found a few more cases of stable goo, some still in pods. Ooh! Do you know about the pods? Bruno will have to tell you. But we've also found a lot of unstable goo, stuff that can't transform. So I conducted some exposure experiments and analysis of the substance. We were able to make some conclusions that might help explain your zoo animals."

The meeting participants settled into their chairs as Cindy

presented her results.

"We first reviewed the recovery logs to see where we found goo... under what conditions, like temperature, how much moisture... stuff like that. And then we reviewed the transformation results. When we found the substance in the hot sun, it didn't transform into a mouse. It was unstable. When we found it on snow or ice, it was unstable. When we found it under cool, wet conditions, like after rain or watering with a sprinkler, the substance was stable and transformed into a mouse.

"I compared stable substance with unstable substance. The unstable substance had a different membrane protein structure than the stable goo. The proteins in the unstable goo were scrambled, which resulted in the inability to transform.

"So we exposed stable goo to various conditions here in the lab to see what denatures the proteins."

"And?"

"Extreme heat, above one hundred degrees denatured the membrane proteins. Extreme cold, below minus twenty denatured the membrane proteins. And low humidity, less than one percent denatured the membrane proteins. But moderate heat and cold did not. Last, but not least, exposure to light... UV radiation... denatured the proteins. It really scrambled 'em." Cindy stopped to as Ted if he was following the results.

"Continue," Ted said.

"We looked at the proteins by peptide mapping. Let me tell you, those were complicated maps. These proteins are huge. This is where it gets interesting. We were able to confirm that samples exposed to UV radiation had the same scrambled protein structure as the unstable samples we recovered in the field... from Oklahoma, New Mexico and Colorado."

"And UV-exposed substance did not transform into a mouse," Sarah added.

"Yeah, that's right," Cindy said. "So we're pretty sure

UV radiation from the sun made the goo unstable."

"So," Ted summarized, "under normal conditions on Earth, the goo is stable as long as it's not exposed to a lot of sunlight or heat."

"Yep."

After taking a moment to contemplate the information, Ted asked, "So what do you think about the dying zoo animals?"

"If sunlight denatures the proteins in the substance, it might also denature the cells of the transformed animals," suggested Sarah.

"You did say that the incidence of dead animals was in the African savannah-type exhibits, not the jungles," noted Bruno. "No trees on the savannah. They were probably saturated with UV radiation. And it's hot, so that doesn't help."

Everyone nodded in agreement.

"Bruno, you were going to tell me about the... pods?" Ted asked.

"Yes sir. We found what we think are the vessels that contain the substance. It's a flexible, gelatin-like sphere. It's actually very similar to a paint ball. The sphere is pretty tough. It can stand a wide range of temperatures without splitting or becoming brittle."

"How does the substance get out of the pod?"

"Water dissolves the pod."

Ted scratched his chin and paused before speaking. "Let me see if I got it. These pods fall from the sky and wait to get wet. When water dissolves the pod, the goo is stable unless it is exposed to lots of sunlight. And the goo just sits and waits for an animal to come in contact. Then it transforms into a copy of the animal. Did I get it right?"

"Uh... yeah," Jim said. "I think you got it."

After taking very brief notes, almost shorthand, Mr. Stevens got up and addressed the group. "Okay. None of this information is to leak out. I want clampdown on all of this. Nothing leaves this building. Goo can come in, but nothing… not even the mice can leave. We have to silently wait. Wait for more animals to 'appear', and probably die before we can understand the magnitude of the situation. I'm guessing we'll have a… what did you call it, an 'outbreak'? In the mean time, try to figure out how these pods got here on Earth."

"We'll try," Jim said. "But we don't really know what we're looking for or where we'll find it.

"We'll know it when we find it," Ted said. "Or we'll know it when someone finds it for us."

Chapter 11 - I'm Scared

David spent the afternoon outside. He didn't do much of anything. He just wanted to be outside.

As the shadows grew longer, he stood in his driveway and stretched. Then he noticed the small girl, his neighbor's daughter, running down the road. He scratched the back of his head. He hadn't seen her run along the road by herself before. He found that odd. He watched as the girl turned into his driveway and ran all the way up to him.

"Mr. David," Karen gasped. "Mr. David... I... I'm scared. I ran. I need your help!!!"

David knew something was very wrong if this girl was at his house asking *him* for help.

"It's my mom!" Karen yelled. "C'mon!!!"

Chapter 12 - What's Your Name?

David and Karen hurried to her house. David had to run at close to his top speed to keep up with the girl. They ran up the driveway and entered through the front door.

They walked into the kitchen and saw a woman sitting in a chair at the table. She appeared to be about thirty years old. She was tall and thin, with long sandy brown hair. And she was naked. She looked up at David and Karen but didn't stand up. She appeared to David to be the mother of the girl, but... he hadn't ever really had an up-close look at her. He couldn't tell for sure.

Realizing the woman's appearance, David apologized for himself and hid his eyes. But it was clear the woman was not embarrassed in the least to be seen without clothes.

"See?" Karen asked David excitedly.

"What?"

"She's just sitting! She doesn't talk! She doesn't know I'm here! She doesn't know me! This is not my mother!"

David stood in the kitchen, confused, looking back and forth from Karen to the woman.

"Mommy!" Karen pleaded with the woman. "What are you doing?"

"Sitting," the woman calmly responded.

Trying a different approach, David asked the woman, "What's your name?"

"Mommy."

"Do you have another name?"

"No," she replied. Then, pointing to Karen, she said, "I don't know her."

David then knew something was very wrong.

Coming toward the house, two voices became audible. "Be reasonable Sue! You must have imagined it," suggested the first. "You've been out in the sun too long."

"I did not imagine it, Petunia!" insisted the other. "She's probably sitting inside right now! Oh God! I hope Karen's alright."

Hearing her mother approaching the house with Mrs. Clark, Karen yelled, "Mommy!"

"Karen! Thank goodness you're okay!" Her mother burst into the house followed by Petunia Clark. They saw the other woman sitting at the table. Karen was standing with the man from across the street.

"David Hudson, ma'am... your neighbor down the road."

Without making any introductions in return, she pointed to the woman. "See? What did I tell you, Petunia?"

Petunia was stunned. Everyone was stunned.

"Who are you?" the naked woman quietly asked her twin.

"Sue," replied Karen's mother.

They all stood in the kitchen staring at the woman, not knowing what to do. They looked to each other, but nothing came to mind. This was a new experience for all of them.

Finally, Karen's mother broke the silence. "Ah! This is ridiculous." Unable to take the sight of herself sitting naked in the kitchen, she walked out of the room. The others just waited for something to happen. Nothing did. The new woman simply sat at the table.

Karen's mother returned with clothes for the woman to wear. "Here, put these on." But the woman did not understand. Karen's mother rolled her eyes and sighed. She had to explain how to put them on and help the woman. She decided to not even bother with a bra; explaining its purpose and trying to tell the woman how to fasten it was well beyond the woman's capacity.

Once the woman was dressed, the others left her in the kitchen and went into the front room. They asked her to stay seated in the kitchen.

David turned to Karen's mother and asked, "What the hell happened... er..."

"Sorry," she apologized. "I'm Susan Roberts. This is my daughter Karen. And this is our neighbor, Petunia Clark."

"Glad to meet you Susan, Karen, Petunia," David said.

Susan started to explain, "I was working in the garden, cleaning up the plants, you know... peppers, beans, tomatoes... pulling them up and putting them on the mulch pile. I was picking up the tomatoes that had fallen under the plants. They're always rotten and squishy, so I didn't notice at first. When I grabbed a few, I distinctly noticed something sticky. Like jam or corn syrup. I had a weird feeling, but... then it vanished. I thought the sticky stuff must have been some really rotten tomatoes, so I just kept walking to the mulch pile and dumped them. I turned around and... there she was! I screamed. I was completely freaked out. Instinctively, I ran to Petunia's house."

"I heard Mommy scream," Karen added. "I went in the kitchen to see what happened. The lady walked into the house and sat down. I tried to talk to her, but she didn't say anything. She just sat there. I got so scared that I ran. I didn't think about where to run. I just ran. I ended up at your house, mister." Looking to her mother, she apologized, "Sorry mommy. I should have gone to Mrs. Clark's house."

"It's okay, honey. You're safe." Susan continued recounting the incident. "I tried to explain what happened to Petunia, but she didn't believe me. Who would? So I dragged her back here... as you saw."

"So you think it was from this sticky stuff that the

woman appeared?" David asked.

"Yeah," Susan replied. "I don't know why, but I think it *was* that sticky stuff that made all this happen."

"I'm gonna call Spike... er... Bill Leland, the deputy sheriff," David told the others. "He came by my house a few days ago and said some weird stuff. He mentioned reports of 'goop' found in the area."

"News of this can't get out!" Susan insisted. "There can't be two of me!"

"What do you propose we do with the second you?" David inquired.

They all thought for a moment or two. No one had an answer.

Susan sighed. "Alright, call him," she said. "But he's gotta keep this secret. No police reports or anything. People can find those, you know. What will people think?" she asked with a worried look on her face.

"Gossip is not the problem," David stated plainly. "A new person is the problem."

David called Spike--he knew how to get a hold of the deputy directly. Spike told David he'd be right over.

The neighbors silently stood in the front room waiting for the deputy to arrive. They didn't really have much to say. The person in the kitchen had left them speechless.

Within five minutes of David's call, the cruiser pulled into Susan's driveway. When Spike entered the front room of the house, they each explained their perspective of the events of the afternoon. Spike listened, not writing down a single word.

After hearing from the four neighbors, he looked at the woman in the kitchen. The others followed him with curiosity. Spike walked around the table and stood in front of her. He asked, "What's your name?"

"Sue."

He asked her age, where she was born, and who her parents were.

The response was the same for each: "I don't know."

Spike and the others returned to the family room. The woman did not follow.

"Okay, here's the deal," Spike said. "There have been reports of a substance that has been found around the U.S. I called it 'goop' when we last talked, David. There are reports of weird stuff, like more zoo animals and more dead ground hogs, field mice, and... *gophers* than there ought to be, but nothing as weird as this. I've got to call this in."

Susan protested, but Spike raised his hand and tried to ease her fears. "Everything will be confidential, Susan. We'll be very careful. This is not a normal report. This will go straight to the Department of Homeland Security. This won't get out." He took a breath. "Now," he said, pointing toward the woman in the kitchen, "what do we do with her?"

Although each seemed to have thoughts about what to do, no one voiced any. Spike told the others "Keep her inside until I hear back from DHS."

"What should we... er... do?" Susan asked.

"Well obviously feed her. After that..." Spike stopped to contemplate what should be done. *The woman didn't seem dangerous. Keep her away from the girl? Probably don't have to. How could we keep them apart? Should we let her do whatever she wants? Watch TV? Read newspapers and books?*

His expression changed from contemplation to concern. "She knew her name, didn't she? Well... your name, right?" he asked Susan. Susan nodded. "That means she can learn. Crap! Did she hear our conversation?" The others shrugged. "Listen... we have to keep her away from sources of information like TV, internet, radio, and newspapers."

Petunia, Susan, and Karen looked terribly confused. David understood. One of his previous "jobs" trained him to know why Spike gave these instructions.

"She listens and observes," Spike said in a quiet voice, so the new woman wouldn't hear. "She's like a child with no knowledge or memory. Her mind is a sponge ready to soak up information. But we can't let her learn anything until we know what the hell she is and why she's here. If she starts watching news, or reading papers, or surfing the internet, she could learn a lot fast."

"Am I supposed to keep her in the coat closet?" Susan asked.

"No, but we have to control the environment," Spike instructed. "We have to get rid of printed news or current events. Give them to someone or burn them. And if you have a computer, put a password on it. And do not give it Karen."

"Why not?" Karen quickly asked, offended.

"Karen, you're a smart girl," Spike told her sincerely. "But that lady may try to ask you for the passwords. Or she may ask questions to try to figure out what the passwords are. It's very important you don't tell her anything."

"Why?"

"You know a lot of things, Karen," Spike continued. "A lot of things the other lady might want to know. She's like a stranger. You don't tell things to strangers, right?"

"Yes, but she's in our house. And she looks like mommy, so she's not a stranger," Karen replied, looking confused. She paused and then suddenly asked, "Hey, how do I tell them apart?"

"Um…" Spike hesitated. He thought about her question, and then came up with a solution. "Susan, you have things that only you two know… things from your past, before *she* showed up today. You'll have to work out a system of security questions for Karen to ask you, like favorite foods or your father's name."

"That should work," Susan responded.

"Yeah, like what I was for Halloween last year," suggested Karen. "I was a farmer. Or you could ask how you carved the pumpkin last year. It was Elmo!"

The optimism of Spike and Susan finding a solution quickly vanished. They both knew Karen would not be able to keep many secrets. Most precocious, out-going six-year-olds cannot.

"You're over-thinking this," David told Spike. He turned to Susan and said, "Cut your hair."

Spike and Susan both rolled their eyes. Susan said, "Duh." They had the solution to telling the two women apart.

"Getting back to sources of information," Spike said, "get rid of what you can. Don't expose her to current events or anything."

"What am I supposed to do with Karen? Can they be together?" Susan asked with concern.

"I think it'll be okay," Spike reassured her.

"Can they watch TV for an hour or two?"

"Do you have cable or satellite? Can you block channels?"

"I already blocked the inappropriate stuff," Susan replied.

"No," Spike interjected. "You have to block news channels, local channels, maybe even sports. You can leave the cartoons and documentaries, but nothing current. Shoot, commercials." He paused to think if ads would be a problem. "Oh well," he concluded, "if the channel is appropriate, the commercials should be okay. We can't do anything about that. You can give her children's books, but nothing more advanced than what Karen's reading."

"So we have to keep her at age six?" Susan asked.

"Yes, until we can figure things out," Spike replied. "I have to leave and go call this in. I'll be in touch. Keep her safe and uneducated. Thanks."

Spike departed, leaving the others to change the environment for the other Sue.

Chapter 13 - Ignorant and Happy

Mr. Stevens took a seat in the conference room and began his briefing for the committee. "Now that a person has appeared, we have to react. If we can't contain it, it might become a national emergency."

The chairman, General Gilmore, said, "Last time you were here, Ted, you said there was nothing to worry about... just a couple stories about more animals than usual. But the public hadn't noticed. 'Let it ride,' you said. Now it's almost an emergency?"

"Yes, that's true," Ted replied. "When I first visited this committee, the scope of the issue was smaller, simply rodents and zoo animals that no one noticed. Now a person has transformed. If additional people transform, or if there are already more out there that the public and local officials are trying to deal with, this whole thing could get out of control quickly. People might panic."

"We have to eliminate the risk to citizens," the general said firmly.

"So you know what causes the transformation?" asked Mr. Mason, a second, committee member. "Is it this substance that you mention in your report, the substance that has been found across the country?"

"Yes."

"And this substance comes in spheres?" Mr. Mason asked. "Can't we round up these spheres and destroy them?"

"We're trying sir, but they're spread out. And the substance is not always still contained in the pods. It's impossible to search for it. That would be a needle in a haystack the size of the U.S. We find the substance when a person discovers a blob or a pod and calls it in. Or we find it when someone calls in an occurrence; when an animal, or now a person, touches it and creates another."

"We cannot just sit on the sidelines and wait for people to stumble upon the substance and make alien copies of them!" the Chairman insisted. "We have to find this stuff!"

"I understand your concern, sir. Honestly, I have the same desire. Protecting our citizens is the most important objective," Ted calmly said. "But it's impossible to comb every square inch of the country looking for pods of goo. We recover pods when we find them. We control the substance when we find it. And we try to keep a lid on the increased number of animals. It's worked up until now."

"And now?" asked Mr. Wright, the third member of the committee.

"Now it looks like we'll have to deal with the new person, or new people, if there are more out there."

"And exactly how do we do that, Ted?" the general snidely asked. "We can't send 'em back!"

"We have considered several possibilities, sir. We can do nothing and let them freely integrate into society."

"Unacceptable! Aliens running around the streets?"

"I agree, sir. That would be too risky. Alternatively, we could kill them."

"Kill them?" Mr. Wright shouted. "Genocide? Are you crazy? We can't just kill people, even if they aren't really people."

"I agree. Of course we cannot kill them," Ted said quietly and slowly to calm Mr. Wright. "But if the public finds out, they might think differently if they know these people are from somewhere other than Earth." He paused to let the committee think. "The third option is to set up an internment camp somewhere in the desert. That way we can house them under controlled conditions. They'll be out of public view and contained." As a side note, he added, "They may also happen to die of natural causes."

"What do you mean?" Mr. Mason asked.

"We know the substance and the animals that transform from it are sensitive to light. The proteins in their cells get all scrambled when exposed to too much sun. That's why we have reports of dead animals in farm fields and in sunny zoo exhibits. Our lab confirmed this. So if we put these people out in the desert, say, in Arizona or California, they might get too much exposure to sun and die."

"Are we just going to throw them in the desert and leave them to die?"

"No, sir," Ted replied to the chairman. "We'll have to house them. We'll give them a place to stay where there's plenty of sunlight and dry conditions. But over time, all that exposure might take its toll."

"Where can we house them?" asked Mr. Mason.

"We have several abandoned military bases. The houses and streets are still there. We can set up the Base Exchange for supplies. We can give the residents books and satellite TV, with restricted programming, of course. We'll keep them contained."

"Any chance they can revolt or riot or escape or anything?" the chairman inquired.

"I don't think so, sir. The person we found had no memory. If we don't give her any information that she can use against us, we should be able to keep her content. If others are discovered and moved in, the people will obviously talk to each other, but if they aren't aware of their situation relative to the rest of society, they won't have any reason to be unhappy."

Mr. Wright chuckled and said, "Ignorant and happy."

The general gave Ted his instructions. "We must make sure we control the information we provide to them. Bring a detailed proposal to us early next week, or sooner. We want to see what we'll provide them, where they'll live, what security will be in place. We want to see everything before we approve it. We can't afford to overlook anything. We have to get moving on this right away, before any more new aliens start appearing." He sat back in his seat and asked, "Now, what do we do with the one we already have?"

Chapter 14 - In Two Days

After school, Karen walked down the road toward her house. She passed the house of Mrs. Clark, but she knew that Mrs. Clark was not home. Mrs. Clark was at Karen's house. Petunia watched the house and the new person while Susan was at work and Karen was at school.

When she entered her house, Karen tossed her backpack aside. The copy of her mother was sitting in the front room with wide eyes, excited. "Hi!" Karen said, as she saw the woman.

"Hi!" Sue replied.

Karen went into the kitchen to get some food. She met Mrs. Clark at the refrigerator. "Hello."

"Good afternoon, Karen." Petunia asked, "Did you have a nice day at school?"

"It was okay. Nothing exciting happened. What about you?"

"I've been here since your mom went to work. Mr. Hudson stopped by for a while in the morning to give me time to run some errands."

"Did anything interesting happen?" Karen asked.

"No. She read three of your books before she got bored. She slept for a while and ate lunch. I think she's excited you're home. Now she can watch TV. I think that's the highlight of her day. Will you be okay until your mom gets home?"

"I think so."

"I'll call or stop by around dinner, okay?"

"Okay. Thanks Mrs. Clark."

Petunia exited the house through the back patio door.

Karen grabbed two juice boxes and two cheese sticks from the refrigerator and moved to the front room to watch TV. It was clear to Karen that the woman was anticipating the afternoon entertainment of SpongeBob and Phineas and Ferb. "Are you ready to watch?" Karen asked. She handed a juice box and cheese stick to Sue.

"Yes, I am," Sue answered. "I like these shows."

As the program started, Karen and Sue both sang, "Oh... Who lives in a pineapple under the sea? Sponge... Bob... Square... Pants!" They both chuckled.

Sitting on the sofa with her eyes on the TV, Karen asked Sue, "Did you have fun today?"

"I did. I learned a lot," Sue replied. "I read the book about the United States and about animals. I like those books. And I read a small book about a moon."

"You probably mean Goodnight Moon," Karen replied.

"Yes."

"That's a book to teach kids how to read or to put you to sleep at night when your mom reads it to you."

"I didn't learn anything from that book. I like the other books better. They're bigger and have more words."

"I like those books, too," Karen told Sue. "I like learning about the planet and the states and animals."

"So do I," replied Sue. "I want to read about the planet also. Can you show me that book?"

"Sure. I'll show you tonight so you can read it tomorrow."

"Thank you," Sue replied with a smile.

The two passed the rest of the afternoon watching cartoons. They were two girls of the same mind. Karen was happy to have Sue in the house. Sue was happy to have Karen teach her.

In the early evening, Karen's mother came home. It was a short drive back to Enterprise from Abilene where she worked as a curator in the Eisenhower Presidential Library.

Karen met her mother in the kitchen while Sue continued watching TV. Karen told her of the day's events at school. While she described the latest antics of Ricky, the doorbell rang. Karen ran to the door and asked who it was. After confirming it was Mrs. Clark, Karen opened the door and invited her in.

As Karen started to close the door, she saw a car pull into her driveway. She waited to see who got out of the car. It was Mr. David and Deputy Leland. Karen watched as they walked up the path to the front door, and she let them inside.

Spike began right away, "Oh good, Petunia, you're here too. Listen, I came to talk to you all. I have some news." He looked at Sue, who was preoccupied with watching TV. "Can we go somewhere out of hearing range?"

"Sure, let's go... let's go out back," suggested Susan.

They followed Karen out the sliding door to the backyard patio. Susan turned the stove off on her way out. Dinner would probably have to wait.

Spike continued, "I heard back from DHS. I know it took a while, but they had to make a lot of plans before doing anything. They had to put a lot of things in place. They're going to move her. They're moving her to a place where they can control her environment."

"Where is that?" Susan asked.

"I don't know. They won't tell me."

"When?"

"In two days, Thursday afternoon, they'll pick her up. Can you come home early, Susan?"

"Yes. I'll be here."

"I want you to be here too, Petunia, and you too, David. They'll probably want to talk to all of you. Of course, I'll be here as well."

"Are you going to take her away?" Karen asked.

Spike nodded.

"But I like her! I don't want her to go!"

"Sweetie, she has to go," her mother told her. "She doesn't belong here with you and me. She's not part of this family. They're going to... uh... take her to her own family."

"They'll take good care of her," Spike reassured Karen. "She'll be with her relatives. Your mom is right, she doesn't belong here."

Chapter 15 – Alien-Made

Dr. Bailey met Mr. Stevens at the front door after he unexpectedly called. "Ted! To what do we owe this honor? Visiting us on a Thursday morning? We didn't even have time to prepare a presentation."

"No need for presentations, Jim. I'm in the area for another call. But I had to stop by and show you something," he said with a sly grin on his face. "Can you get Bruno and the other group leaders?"

"Sure. Let me call them." He picked up the phone and paged Bruno. Jim told him to get Cindy and Sarah and join him in the conference room. "They'll be right up. So... what does your family think of you traveling so much?" Jim asked, filling time while they waited.

"I don't have a family. I'm married to the Department."

"Um..."

"Don't worry, Jim," Ted told him with a smile. "I'm not offended."

Bruno, Sarah, and Cindy joined the two men in the visitor's conference room.

"Doctor Jones!" Ted called out. "Come over here and look at what I have." Bruno and the others crowded around Ted. He took a round rock, a bit larger than a softball, out of a brown paper bag. It looked like a perfect sphere of marble. "This is a meteorite that landed in Nebraska. A woman found it. She happened to see it land," he said with a wicked smile, "right through the vinyl top of her new convertible." He laughed, imagining the shock of the woman seeing her punctured car roof.

"The fire department responded to extinguish her burning upholstery. The station chief was on the call that day and saw the meteorite. He said it didn't really look like a meteorite. He heard about the goo on the DHS network, so he thought it might be related, or at least worth investigating further. He called his friend, the Chief of Police, who took it to a friend, a local college geologist. The geologist took a few minutes to look it over and concluded it was not a random hunk of rock from space. It was a perfect sphere. All diameter measurements he made were exactly the same. The surface of the meteorite was entirely smooth, as if glazed, like pottery. The geologist was absolutely certain it was not natural. The meteorite was man-made."

"Or alien-made," Jim added.

"Apparently," Ted acknowledged. "Let's cut it open and see what's inside," he said with anticipation.

"I'll bet you ten dollars there's a pod inside," Sarah excitedly offered Ted.

"Okay," Ted happily replied. "I'll take that bet."

"Let's go to the lab!" Bruno called as he sprang to his feet. He and Mr. Stevens practically skipped with excitement to the lab. The others followed with a little less enthusiasm. They entered a storage room containing tools and hardware, beakers and flasks. Mr. Stevens placed the meteorite on the counter for Bruno. "Uh... what should I use to open it?" Bruno asked Ted. "Do I need to be careful?"

"What would you normally use to split a rock?"

"I guess a chisel. I think we have one in here somewhere."

Bruno found the old rusty chisel and a hammer. He stabilized the meteorite with four rubber stoppers and carefully placed the chisel at the top. He squinted, raised the hammer, and struck the chisel. The meteorite cracked from top to bottom, all the way around. With one additional light tap of the chisel, the rock split in two hemispheres. One half contained a clear, flexible sphere: a pod.

"Alright, ten bucks!" Sarah shouted.

"Sarah, Cindy… please take the pod to the lab and conduct the usual analyses," Jim instructed. "Bruno, let's see what we can find out about this meteorite."

"Jim, Doctor Jones, Cindy, Sarah… I will leave you to your work. I got the answer I was looking for. Oh yeah, here's ten dollars for each of you." He handed Jim two twenties. "I have my other appointment to go to." Ted turned to leave and added, "I'll let myself out if that's okay. Thanks."

"I'll phone you, Ted, as soon as we learn anything," Jim told him.

"Just invite me back, Jim. No need to give any details when you call. I'll be happy to return in person to hear the latest."

As the afternoon turned to dusk, Ted pulled into the driveway of Susan and Karen's house. Deputy Leland arrived in his sheriff's cruiser with David in the passenger seat. The three men got out of their cars and walked up the path to the house together.

Karen opened the door for them. They entered and Spike made all the introductions.

Ted began, "Thank you, Ms. Roberts, for your patience and understanding. I can hardly imagine how this has affected you and Karen. And I understand from Deputy Leland that you, Mrs. Clark, and you, David, have been quite helpful to keep this quiet and assist with observation duties." They nodded. "This has been something that no one was prepared for. I hope we can bring this to a conclusion for you," Ted said with a smile. "Now, I cannot share too much with you about the future plans for her, but I can take questions if you have them. I'll answer what I can."

"Where is Sue going?" Karen asked. "What will happen to her? Will she be joining her relatives?"

"The lady that has been staying with you is going to a new home. We've made it special for her. She's going to live there instead of here. We've found some of her relatives." He glanced around at the adults, indicating additional new people had been cloned. He looked back to Karen and continued, "But her family is spread out over the country, so it will be a little while before any relatives join her."

Petunia asked, "What will she do during the day if none of her relatives will be there to keep her company?"

"We'll have friends keep an eye on her, just like Karen did," Ted said.

"Can I write her a letter?" Karen asked.

"I think you'll be able to," he told her. "I don't know what her address will be yet, so I'll have to get that for you."

Karen smiled at his response.

Looking to the adults, he asked, "Any other questions?" He paused and looked at each person. "No? Okay, let's get her."

Susan led Ted down the hall to Karen's room where their guest was waiting. The door was closed. Mr. Stevens knocked lightly.

"Come in," replied Sue.

Ted opened the door and entered the room. "Hello ma'am. My name is Mr. Stevens. I have been asked to escort you to your new home. Ms. Roberts and her daughter have enjoyed your visit, but it's time to take you on a trip. We'd like to give you your own house. How does that sound?"

"I like it here. Will I like it there?" Sue asked.

"I think so," Ted replied with a smile, trying to be reassuring. "We'll have many things for you to do. And you will have your own house. Perhaps you'd like a pink room like this, with animal pictures on the wall."

"I think I would."

"The airplane that will take you to your new home will depart in about an hour. Are you ready to leave?"

"Karen explained that I must go away. She doesn't know why. You said I will have a new home. Why?"

Ted paused a moment, thinking of how to explain the situation. He then told Sue, "When you arrived here, you arrived as a guest. But this house belongs to Karen and her mother. This is not your house. You need your own house, a place to live."

"I would like to live with Karen and her mother. Karen is my sister."

"Karen is actually a friend," Ted replied. "She's a friend you have been visiting for a while. But now it's time to go to your home."

Sue did not reply.

"Are you ready to leave?" Ted asked cautiously.

Sue thought for a few seconds and then nodded.

"Please follow me," Ted told her.

When Sue stood up, the others backed down the hall and waited in the front room. Petunia, David, and Susan all awkwardly said goodbye to their guest.

Karen approached Sue and hugged her. "Goodbye, Sue. Have fun at your new house. I'll miss you. I'll send you letters, okay?"

"I'd like that. Thank you," Sue said with a smile, looking into Karen's eyes. "Mr. Stevens says I'm a guest, visiting you. But I think you're my sister. I liked learning with you, and reading your books, and watching TV with you. I'll miss you, Karen."

Karen smiled in return, looking back at Sue, and her eyes filled with tears. "I'll miss you, too."

"Thank you all, again, for everything you have endured," Ted said to Susan, Petunia, and David. "I will keep you updated, probably through Deputy Leland. Ms. Roberts, I hope you don't mind that we are taking the outfit of yours that she happens to be wearing tonight."

Susan shook her head with a restrained smile.

"I think I have disturbed you all quite enough. I shall take my leave. Mrs. Clark, David, Karen, Ms. Roberts, goodnight to you all. Deputy, can I have a quick word with you outside?"

"Sure, Ted." Looking to the others, Spike added, "I'll say goodnight to you all as well." He and Mr. Stevens and exited the house, escorting Sue.

Sue waved to Karen as she left the house. Karen waved back.

Susan locked the front door as it closed, and leaned her back against it with a sigh. "Thank God this whole thing is over and we'll never see that woman again."

Chapter 16 - Survival

Dr. Bailey brought a treat for everyone in the lab. He called Cindy first to tell her to spread the word that doughnuts were in the front conference room. He did not need to lift a finger to dial another number; everyone in the building came up to the conference room within a couple minutes. His heart filled with pride to know how well all of his analysts communicated with each other--even if it was only about doughnuts.

Talking loud over the excitement, Jim addressed the analysts with a big smile, "Good morning!"

Everyone replied by raising their doughnuts and saying something inaudible, since their mouths were full.

"I want to thank you all for your hard work, particularly over the past few weeks. This whole lab has generated results that are truly earth-changing. You have performed work that most labs in the world will never perform. And although no one knows what we do here, we know. We know the importance of our analyses and the results. I think you are the best group anyone could hope to work with. Thank you!"

Applause erupted from the group as the analysts celebrated.

Dr. Bailey walked among his employees, talking sincerely with each. He knew each analyst and could have easy discussions with all.

Everyone appreciated the time Dr. Bailey routinely took to walk through the lab and talk with everyone. He understood the analyses that each person conducted. He could discuss results with each analyst and helped them understand how the results fit into the larger picture. He was well-liked by all. Doughnuts certainly didn't hurt his reputation.

As the lab enjoyed the Monday morning breakfast festivities, Dr. Bailey's call phone rang. A visitor arrived. Jim left the room to let his guest into the building.

Mr. Stevens entered the conference room with Dr. Bailey and observed the assembly. The analysts closest to the door saw Mr. Stevens and began to settle down. The subdued mood spread like a wave through the room.

"No no no!" Ted said quickly, waving his hands. "Please don't stop. I don't want to break up this party." Thinking he had irreparably damaged the mood, he added, "In fact, I came here to thank you and let you all know I've made arrangements to provide a catered lunch for everyone in the lab. Just name the day and it'll be here."

That worked. The room erupted in applause and cheering.

Ted continued above the noise. "I just want to say that my office is so pleased with the efficiency that this lab generates results. We are so much further along in our investigation because of this lab. Thank you all!"

Mr. Stevens took a seat on a chair he found in the corner. He just sat and waited. He was more than happy to wait while the assembly broke up naturally.

Once the group's collective sugar rush subsided, the analysts filtered back to their labs. Mr. Stevens approached Dr. Bailey and pleasantly asked if he could have a few minutes with him and his group leaders.

The group leaders returned to the conference room and

Mr. Stevens began the impromptu meeting. With a relaxed smile, he said, "Sorry for the unannounced visit. But I am sure that you have some answers already. I hope I'm correct."

"You must be racking up the frequent flyer miles. Two visits in four days?" Sarah asked.

"Actually, some of my staff and I have been staying in a hotel in town for a few days. The meteorite, your lab's continued analyses, and the other business I had to attend to in the area are the most important details in this whole affair. They've required most of my attention. Now, let's talk about the meteorite."

"Well..." Bruno began, "after we spilt the sphere on Thursday, I tried to establish the nature of the rocky material. Unfortunately, we don't have a lot of experience with rocks. We're a biological lab, not geological. But I was able to find a simple test to compare density of rocks. It's a water absorption test. You basically dry the rock sample in an oven with low heat. Then you weigh it. After soaking it in water for twenty-four hours, you re-weigh the sample. The more porous the material, the more water it will absorb. Porcelain is the least porous... absorbing less than one half percent of its weight. Ceramic can absorb up to four percent. Terra cotta and lava rocks absorb even more. Our meteorite was definitely in the porcelain family."

"What advantage does porcelain have over more porous material?" Ted asked.

"It's fired at a much higher temperature... more than three thousand degrees. Its lower porosity gives it strength and heat tolerance. Material fired at lower temperatures, like earthenware or terra cotta are brittle. For comparison, the tiles on the space shuttle were ceramic. They worked quite well to dissipate re-entry heat from the shuttle. The meteorite you gave us was made with porcelain-like material, probably to protect it during re-entry through an atmosphere as thick as ours."

"The pod recovered from the meteorite was in perfect

condition," Cindy told Ted. "It was still flexible and completely clear. And the substance inside was the same as the other stable samples. Since it was so well-protected, it's basically the best sample we have."

"And it transformed mice just like the other stable goo," Sarah added.

"Okay," Ted said, guiding the discussion down a new course, "let's think about where this meteorite came from."

The group leaders shifted in their seats uncomfortably. They weren't prepared to discuss from where the meteorite arrived.

Seeing their hesitation, Ted reassured the analysts and challenged them. "Look, I understand you're biologists and biochemists, but you're scientists. And you're all pretty smart, so let's do a little brainstorming to see what we can come up with."

"Well…" Jim began slowly, "because we found the meteorite which, we presume, actually came from space, we basically confirmed the substance and pods are not from this planet."

"That's easy to conclude," Ted noted. "Anything else?"

"Given the thickness of the meteorite, it was designed specifically to protect the pod," Jim continued.

"But it would have to break open to release the pod to release the substance," added Bruno.

"So… it would have to be thick enough to travel through an atmosphere, but not too thick," Ted confirmed. "If it was too thick it wouldn't break up."

After a pause, Jim suggested, "It might have been specifically designed for Earth, for our atmosphere."

"But the meteorite did not break apart," Sarah noted.

"Maybe the aliens didn't anticipate convertible tops and bucket seats that would cushion the fall," Bruno joked.

"Ha ha," Sarah responded with a smirk. "Maybe there are meteorites of different thicknesses to give an increased probability of success. Instead of all your eggs in a basket of one thickness, make eggs of variable thicknesses to increase the odds of making it through the atmosphere and splitting open upon impact. This egg didn't break, but others may have broken or shattered when they hit the ground."

"You should have seen remnants of these 'eggs' when you found pods and goo, correct?" Ted asked. "Did you?"

The three group leaders looked nervously at each other.

"If you didn't, I need to know it. You're not on trial," Ted told them.

Jim supported his people by explaining to Ted, "I don't think our teams looked carefully enough to answer this question. We can review our recovery logs, but I'm not aware of specific observations about cracked ceramic eggs in the vicinity."

"Okay, no big deal," Ted said calmly. "Review the logs to see if there's anything there."

"Hold on," Bruno interjected. "If these things are coming in from space, they're moving fast, right? And they're still hot, right? So they're at their most fragile state, right? So maybe there won't be any debris when they hit because they shatter. No egg shells to even see."

"Maybe that explains why there was no debris around the goo we found," Cindy added. "There was nothing to see because the eggs shattered. That's why the substance was a blob of goo and not in a pod. It didn't stand a chance to stay in the pod."

"What about the intact pods you found?" Ted asked. "Any sign of shells?"

"What if the egg split in half?" Sarah thought out loud. "If the egg split, the pod could have rolled out and kept rolling away from the egg."

"Eh... It's a convenient explanation," Ted said skeptically. "I'm not saying it's incorrect, but highly convenient." He pointed in Jim's general direction and told him, "You should start keeping an eye out for more perfectly spherical ceramic meteorites, you think?"

"That would make sense," Jim replied.

Mr. Stevens continued, "So we have eggs of different

thicknesses that have been sent to Earth. And these eggs contain pods of goo that transforms into Earth's indigenous animals. Why?"

Each scientist sat in silence. It was as if they had been asked the meaning of life.

"How could this whole thing make sense?" Ted asked.

"This is some really deep stuff you're asking us," Sarah said.

"Yes, I can see how explaining the purpose of transforming alien goo arriving in pods from space could be considered 'deep', but humor me."

"Well…" Sarah began slowly, trying to piece it together, "if they sent actual alien beings it would be… like… an invasion, right?"

"Presumably," agreed Ted, "unless they just wanted to get some Starbucks." He couldn't help but laugh out loud at his own joke.

The others laughed too. It was a good one.

"But sending goo that transforms into Earth's animals would… um… add to the planet's population," Sarah continued. "What good would that do? It's not like Earth's rats can build a spaceship and go back home or attack another planet."

"It's not a means of procreating," Cindy said. "They're not increasing their own population."

"Then why do it?" Ted asked.

More silence.

"C'mon! Work with me people." Ted pushed the analysts harder. "No one else in DHS has enough brains to even contemplate half the stuff that you know. Why would an alien species send transforming goo to another planet just so it can transform into that planet's own species?"

Still silence, but at least Mr. Stevens could see the scientists were thinking. And they were thinking hard. After several moments, Dr. Bailey suggested, "Survival."

"Explain."

"Transforming into another species is better than dying

out completely. Maybe the cellular substance is a way to survive," suggested Jim.

"But the substance doesn't retain any alien... anything," Cindy argued. "It transforms into a normal Earth animal, not an alien."

"Not much advantage in that, is there?" Ted concluded.

"You're right," Bruno concurred. "What good is it? It's not invading a competing planet or eliminating a competing species. And it's not increasing its own population. That's like... a disadvantage. Dumb, really."

More thoughtful silence followed. It was broken by Sarah. "You said 'a normal animal'." The others all looked at Sarah. "How do we know the transformed animals are normal? How do we know they don't have some sort of mutation or programming that would either compete with, or eliminate other Earth animals?"

"Why do we assume it's a competition?" asked Cindy. "Maybe it's less direct. If there is some sort of mutation or programming, the species may eventually evolve into the alien species."

"Assuming normal biology," Jim said, "it would take thousands of generations to evolve into a new species."

"Or maybe the programming isn't evolutionary," Sarah proposed. "Maybe it's a message."

"A message? Hold on," Bruno called out. "All of this assumes there's genetic material hidden in the goo. Have we found DNA? Is there a genome hiding in the cellular proteins? Until we find something, we can't say anything about mutations or programming."

"It sounds like you've identified the next phase of this investigation," replied Ted.

Jim responded, "We'll start looking for DNA."

"Good. Now, let me see if I can summarize everything to date. Ceramic eggs--"

"More like porcelain."

"Thank you, Doctor Jones," Ted replied. "Porcelain eggs have fallen through Earth's atmosphere like meteorites.

Inside the eggs are pods containing a gooey substance. When the pod is breached by water, the exposed substance can transform into an animal if one should happen to come in contact with the goo. However, the substance and the transformed animals are not stable when exposed to significant levels of UV radiation from the sun. Exactly why the substance has arrived on Earth cannot be determined at this time." He paused to reflect on what he just said. "Wow," he said, shaking his head. "This gets weirder every week. The half-wits in the Department are not gonna believe this for a minute."

He put his notes into his portfolio and addressed the scientists with a smile, "Thank you all for your time and the discussion. It truly was most valuable. As I said before, no one else has enough intelligence to take your results and try to make sense out of it. I hope that I have not consumed too much of your time this morning. Good Lord! It's ten thirty! I've got to go."

He stood up to leave. "Please look into the DNA programming possibilities. I will be anxious to see if you can find an explanation for this whole thing. And as usual, please keep everything confidential. Thank you." He turned to leave, and then stopped. He added, "Oh yeah... Jim, make sure to send me a text message for which day you'd like lunch catered. I'll have it all arranged for you."

Dr. Bailey walked him out to the front door while the others waited in the conference room. The two men shook hands and said goodbye. The scientists all watched Mr. Stevens walk to his car.

Before getting in, Ted turned to face the building and waved.

Chapter 17 - Their End Game

Mr. Stevens took a seat in front of the committee. "Good afternoon, gentlemen," he began firmly with a straight face. "Last time I was here I laid out the details for housing the new people. I'm here to give you an update. The base has been prepared per the conditions we outlined in our proposal. We've brought in supplies and hired the support staff and counselors. We're in the process of moving the people now. We've identified three adults and two children so far; two women, one man, and two boys. We're bringing them individually to Colorado first and putting them up in a hotel, before moving them all to the base at the same time. We're on schedule to move them in two days. I'll assist with the move personally. We'll fly them to the base in the morning, process them, and assign housing. We'll introduce the staff and explain the boundaries and the amenities."

"What will you tell them when they ask why they're isolated and contained?" asked Mr. Mason.

"First, they have no prior memory. And they're pretty confused right now. Hopefully they don't really know how they came into existence," Ted told the men. "They should be susceptible to suggestion and open to believing what they hear. So we plan to tell them we're establishing a new town. It's the first phase of a government-sponsored project. They have been selected to be the initial residents of the new community. If they believe us, we should be able to answer any other questions they'll have."

"What about the children?" asked Mr. Wright. "They have likely been exposed to other children. How will they adjust to being placed in a new town alone... without people they know? Will they believe the story?"

"I think so," Ted replied. He paused and looked down. "I hope so."

"You hope?" Mr. Wright asked.

"Again, they have no prior memory. So they don't know how children should be raised. And since they appeared from nowhere, they didn't exactly have a warm reception. We plan to convince them it's like camp. The two boys will live in the same house with a rotating crew of counselors. I don't think they'll be homesick or anything like that. They didn't have a home... until now."

"And the housing for the adults?" Mr. Mason asked.

"Each adult will each have their own residence. We hope they settle in make the houses their homes."

"And the entertainment options... same as we discussed before?" confirmed the chairman.

"Yes. Each house has a TV, DVD player, and satellite programming. We've blocked all the news, documentaries and any channel that might feed them information. There aren't many channels available, but hopefully they won't notice. The BX will be stocked with movies they can check out. We've screened them all. And we've also got a library of appropriate books to read. As time goes on, we might be able to expand the options."

"What's our end game?" General Gilmore asked. "What happens one, five, or ten years from now? Do we contain them forever?"

"We contain them for now. We keep these people away from normal citizens. In the future... we don't exactly know. It depends on how the new people react. It depends on how they learn and adapt. It depends on how long they live. It depends on how many we eventually have to contain."

"What's their end game?" Mr. Wright asked. "Why are they here? What do they intend to do?"

"We don't know. Right now, all we know is an alien substance has arrived here on Earth and is increasing our indigenous population. What purpose or advantage that has, we cannot determine at this time. Maybe later, as we observe the new people, a motive will emerge."

"Do either of you have any other questions for Mr. Stevens?" the chairman asked the other two. He paused and waited for a response. "No? Okay. Good luck Ted. We wish you success with the relocation and containment. As usual, please keep this committee updated."

Chapter 18 - Our New Town

Three weeks before the residents moved in, the abandoned air force base in Southeast California was exactly that: abandoned. The cluster of base housing hadn't been used for twenty years. Streets were sun-bleached and cracked. Weeds grew wherever they wanted. Apart from a few broken windows, the houses appeared to be structurally sound. The Base Exchange, or BX in military-speak, was boarded up. Presumably it was as empty as the houses. The razor-wire fences around the entire base prevented anyone from getting in, so the site was undisturbed. A thick layer of grayish-brown desert dust covered everything. The base itself was camouflaged in the desert.

By the day of relocation, the streets had been repaired and repaved. Lawns had been replanted. A cluster of houses near the BX had been cleaned, repaired, and re-painted. The BX had been cleaned, re-painted, re-stocked, and re-opened. Preparations were complete for the arrival of the new residents.

The private jet arrived just after 9:00 am. A cloud of dust was kicked up as it landed on the airfield. When the plane came to a stop at the far end of the runway, a large white van arrived to transport the travelers. The five new residents, two women in khaki shorts and navy blue shirts, and a man wearing a black suit and carrying a black portfolio emerged from the plane and got into the van.

The van drove out of the airfield to the BX. When it came to a stop, the travelers got out. Five other people were standing in front of the building, waiting.

Mr. Stevens walked to the entrance, turned and addressed the assembled people. "Good morning! Welcome to your new home!" He said with a smile. "I'd like to formally introduce you to each other if you haven't already done so. Starting from my left, this is Sue."

Sue timidly waved to the group.

"And this is Donald."

Donald was in his late twenties. He was not particularly handsome, but not unattractive either. He was tall and skinny, but not buff. He made eye contact with the others when he was introduced by Ted and, like Sue, hesitantly waved to the others.

"Next to Donald is Martha."

Martha was very shy. She barely raised her head high enough to look at Ted. Looking at her, you would have guessed she was a mother, or maybe a grandmother. Her hair was graying, but she didn't look very old. She was around five feet tall, but it was hard to tell with her head down. She was not comfortable meeting new people.

"Welcome Martha," Ted said. "Now, this young man," he continued, addressing the younger of the two boys, "is Tyler. He's eight years old."

Tyler had curly blonde hair and blue eyes. He seemed tall for his announced age. He smiled at everyone and waved. Unlike Martha, he was comfortable and happy to meet new people.

"And this fine youth," Ted motioned to the other boy, "is Zachary. He's almost twelve."

Zachary was far less comfortable than Tyler. He kept his head down as he raised his eyes to look at people through the long black hair in his face. He shuffled his feet and lifted his hand to acknowledge the others.

Ted continued, "Thank you all for being patient as we moved you to your new home. All of us here hope you will be comfortable. Let me introduce your community support staff. You have already met Mary and Denise. They were on the plane with you."

Mary was approaching retirement age. She had graying, short curly hair. She always has a pleasant look on her face. She looked like a school teacher or a nurse, which was appropriate since she was a nurse at a teaching hospital before she was given this assignment.

Denise was nearly thirty years old. She was tall with long straight brown hair. If she hadn't been wearing the khaki shorts and blue shirt, "the uniform" as she called it, she would have been wearing the latest west-coast fashions. She, like Mary, looked ready to assist the new residents however they needed.

Ted continued the introductions. "And the other two staff members are Carl and Juliana."

Carl was average. He was middle aged, of average height and average weight. He was balding, but didn't care. Carl was the administrator; a project manager. He knew that Ted relied on him to make sure things ran smoothly.

Juliana could have been Denise's younger sister. She, too, had long straight brown hair. She was as uncomfortable in her khaki shorts and blue shirt as Denise, if not more. She definitely preferred wearing more trendy clothes. She smiled at each of the residents, one at a time, with a nod and a wave.

"They'll all be working here at the Exchange. They will be able to help you with whatever you need," Ted said. "And over here we have the people I hope you two boys will get to know well," he said, addressing Zachary and Tyler. "These young men will be your counselors in your cabin. They are Cody, TJ, and Blake."

The three counselors were nearly mirror images of each other. They looked out of place in their khakis and polo shirts. They should have been wearing board shorts, t-shirts, and surf sandals. They had to be "cleaned up" a bit when they took the assignment, but their hair was still longer than either Ted or Carl would have liked.

"In a few minutes we'll take you all inside the Exchange and let you look around. We'd like to ask you a few questions, and then we'll give you the keys to your new homes. How does that sound?"

Some of the new residents weakly nodded their heads. Moving to the base was yet another new experience to which they had to adjust. They were mostly overwhelmed.

"Any questions before we go in?"

"Will I be returning to the house?" asked Sue.

"To Karen's house, do you mean?" Ted asked. Sue nodded. "No. That was Karen and her mother's house. We're giving you your own house here. I think you'll like it, Sue. You can decorate it any way you'd like. I think I remember you prefer a pink bedroom?"

Sue hesitantly smiled.

"What about Mrs. Philips and Billy? Will they be moving here too?" Tyler asked.

"No. They live back in Maryland. You will be living in this new town with Zachary and the counselors."

"What is the name of this place?" Donald asked. "Where are we?"

"We're further west from where you all were previously. And this town has no name yet. Just like explorers or pioneers, you five, who are the founders of this town, can name it whatever you want. We'll let you decide. Now, shall we get out of the sun and go inside?"

They all entered the Exchange. It was a warehouse with no walls. Only a small portion at the front was occupied with shelves, along with display refrigerators and freezers. There were sections of the shelves for books, movies, food, personal care items, and clothes.

Mr. Stevens continued the orientation, "Please, take a look around. The Exchange is where you will get your food and other household supplies. If you have any questions at all, please contact one of the support staff members. We'll answer your questions as best as we can. If you have any requests for items you can't find, please let us know." He paused and let the new residents look around to take in the surroundings. "While you all look around and get familiar with everything here, Carl will be asking each of you some questions for our files. Sue, would you please start with Carl?"

Sue obliged and accompanied Carl to a table and chairs off to the side. They sat down. Carl took out a pad of paper and began. "Good morning, Sue. Do you have another name... a last name?"

"Sue Roberts."

"Do you know the location or the address of your old house?"

"Yes, number nine, South Grant Street in Enterprise Kansas."

Carl looked up, somewhat startled. He did not expect that much detail.

"That's what was printed on the mail that arrived each day," she added.

"Were there other family members in the residence?"

"Susan, the other Sue, and her six year old daughter named Karen. She's very smart."

"Were there others near the residence that had seen you or talked to you?"

"There were three others. Petunia Clark is the neighbor on Grant Street. She's a nice lady and very helpful to Susan. David Hudson is also a neighbor. He's smart. And there's Deputy Bill Leland, call him Spike."

"While you were at the residence, what did you do during the day?"

"I watched television with Karen when she got home from school. That was the best part of the day. I enjoyed those programs. While Karen was at school, I read her books. I read lots of books. Sometimes I watched the food

TV with Petunia."

"Did you read or view other information?"

"There was nothing else to view. I did not have access to the computer. Once I did view the contents of a... catalog. I think it was called Land's End. It was clothes... not very good."

"Would you prefer to watch television here at your new home?"

"Yes, I'd like to watch the shows I watched before. They're funny. And maybe some new shows, too. I watched a happy man cooking food while people in the room watched him. That was fun. I'd like to watch that too. I would also like to read. I like reading. I liked the animal books and the books about Earth."

"Very good, thank you. Are there any special things you would like in your house?"

"I don't think so," Sue replied.

"Okay, that's all the questions I have right now," Carl told her. "Now, for your new house... here is the key to the door. Do you know how to use a key?"

"Yes, I do."

"Good. You will live in house number one on Second Street. That house is across the street," he said, pointing to the front entrance, "across Main Street from this Exchange. The others will be in houses close to you. Do you have any other questions?"

"I don't think so."

"Thank you, Sue," Carl said.

Sue stood and joined the others touring the Exchange. Mr. Stevens brought Martha over to answer Carl's questions. Martha sat in the chair opposite Carl.

When Martha sat down, Carl motioned to Ted, stood up, and pulled him aside. "Sue knows the house address. She interacted with the neighbors and she watched TV," he whispered. "I think she was pretty well contained, but she did learn... probably more than we would have wanted."

"Carl, we cannot delude ourselves into thinking they have

all been completely isolated and unexposed. We knew some of this already. Yes, they have learned some things. And they will learn more. But we have to control it from here on out. As long as they don't understand how to independently function outside these gates, we'll meet our objective. Now is not the time to panic. Please continue with the interviews."

Carl nodded, sat back at the table opposite Martha, and continued interviewing.

Mr. Stevens re-joined the group to observe the new residents. Donald and Sue were in the middle of a conversation with Denise and Juliana at the freezer.

"And there are pizzas and prepared meals that you can cook in the oven," Denise said.

"What do you mean?" asked Donald.

"Cook means to prepare or heat up. These are really cold to keep them fresh. You can't eat them while they are frozen. You will have to heat these up in an oven to make them hot," explained Juliana.

"I saw Emeril Live do that!" Sue added excitedly. "He places the food in one oven, then pulls it out of another and it's done. I want to try that! I want to cook."

Denise and Juliana chuckled and smiled at Sue. Realizing they had more teaching to do, Denise delayed the discussion by telling Sue, "We'll arrange for cooking lessons starting this afternoon. We'll give you more details and instructions then."

"Can I have my clothes cleaned?" Sue asked, not necessarily intending to change the subject. It was just her next question. "I've been wearing them for a few days."

"Absolutely," Juliana replied. "We have washers and dryers here for your clothes. And please feel free to pick out new clothes from the racks over there. You can select two or three new outfits."

Martha returned to the group and Donald was called by Carl. Martha joined Sue to pick out new clothes. As the women proceeded to the clothes racks, Mary joined them to assist. They crossed paths with Tyler and Zachary, escorted by the counselors. The boys were talking loud and excitedly. The counselors were making a good first impression with the boys.

Mary found several clothing options for Sue and Martha, and in no time they had five or six outfits to try on. They moved to the area at the end of the racks where two dressing rooms had been set up. Sue stopped suddenly and whispered to Martha. The two returned to the racks, smiling and giggling, and selected undergarments.

During the half hour while the women were distracted by trying on clothes, Donald returned from answering Carl's questions and talked with Juliana and Denise, who were in the book and movie section. Donald asked what each movie was about and soon got frustrated when the two staff members evaded his questions. "I'd like to know what this movie is about. Please tell me the story."

Juliana tried to calm him. "Donald, we could tell you the story, but that would not be enjoyable for you. If you know how the movie progresses, it won't be a surprise. The fun in watching a movie is to let the story play out and be surprised at the end." She stood in front of him with her hand on his arm and asked, "Would you skip to the last page of a book and read it to find out how the story ends before you read the whole book?"

"I don't know. I never read a book before."

"Donald, trust us," Denise said with a smile. "Take a movie home with you and watch it. Let the movie tell the story. It will be enjoyable. Trust us."

"Okay," he replied skeptically. "I will."

Sue and Martha emerged from the dressing rooms. They giggled together like a pair of high school friends. They decided to take all of the outfits.

The women walked to the front of the building and met the others who were waiting at the entrance. Donald had a movie and a change of clothes. The boys had snack foods and an eclectic mix of shorts, long-sleeved shirts, black socks and sandals. Mr. Stevens eyed the counselors suspiciously, wondering if the clothes selection was based on current trends or simply to make the boys look weird.

"Please make sure you show all of your items to Carl," Ted instructed the residents. "We'd like to keep an inventory of the things you prefer. We encourage you to visit the Exchange every day. So you only need to take what you need for a day or two."

Sue and Martha looked somewhat ashamed as they held several sets of clothes, but yet, could not hide their enthusiasm.

Mr. Stevens saw the two, smiled, and said, "You may take more than one set of clothes with you. Those do not have to be exchanged every day, nor do you only need one outfit per day," he said, winking at Sue and Martha. "I think a little variety is quite acceptable."

Sue and Martha smiled back at Ted.

"Regarding the other items such as books or movies, we encourage you to share with your neighbors. I imagine that you can also take turns cooking meals for each other and watching movies or television together in your houses."

Sue's face lit up at his first suggestion.

"Now... I understand you'll be having a cooking lesson later. Sue, I hear you are an aspiring chef. Would you be so gracious as to host the cooking party?"

"I'd like to host the cooking party," she said, smiling.

"Excellent. Now, as much as I would love to stay and receive the cooking lesson with you all, I must leave. I wish you good cooking. And remember, please do not hesitate to ask one of the staff members if you need anything. At least one person will be available at all times, day or night, here in the Exchange. And at least one counselor will be with the boys at all times. I hope you will enjoy your new community. I will see you all soon. Goodbye."

Mr. Stevens turned and left the Exchange. He got into the van and rode off to the air field where the waiting jet would take him to his next appointment.

Chapter 19 – My Person

Juliana and Denise arrived at Sue's house with bags of food around 1:00 pm. Martha and Donald were already there. Tyler, Zachary, and TJ knocked a minute later.

"Okay, now that we're all here, let's get cooking," Denise said.

"We thought we'd start with something simple for you all," Juliana told the residents. "Are you familiar with pizza?"

Each resident nodded.

Tyler added, "Sausage and mushrooms are my favorite!"

"There are many kinds of pizza," Denise said. "There's thin crust, thick crust, stuffed crust, regular crust, French bread... all kinds. And you can get many toppings. To make things easy tonight, we brought regular crust pizzas. We have a cheese pizza, a sausage pizza, a pepperoni pizza and a deluxe pizza. Now, Donald, would you like to read the cooking instructions?" She handed him a pizza.

"Okay. It says... um... where are the instructions?"

Denise walked over to Donald and looked over his shoulder. "Let me see... oh, here they are. Wow. These are difficult to read, aren't they?" she asked.

Donald started reading, "Remove the pizza from the

plastic wrapper. Preheat the oven to four thousand F. Place the pizza on the middle rack of the oven and bake for one seven dash one nine minutes."

Juliana smiled and chuckled. "Where you read 'four thousand F', is the last zero smaller than the others and raised higher?" she asked Donald.

"Yes."

"That small zero is a degree symbol," she explained. "So what looks like four thousand F is actually four hundred degrees on the Fahrenheit temperature scale. Most food will cook at temperatures between three hundred fifty and four hundred degrees."

"And the dash is a hyphen to indicate a range of values," Denise added. "So these instructions say you should cook the pizza for seventeen minutes to nineteen minutes."

"Which?" Sue asked, "Seventeen minutes or nineteen minutes? How do we know?"

"We'll look at the pizza and see if it's done after baking for seventeen minutes. If it looks like it should cook longer, we'll leave it for another two minutes," Denise replied.

"Sue, would you like to turn your oven on?" Juliana suggested.

"Yes. How?"

"Press the button that says 'Bake'. The number three hundred fifty should flash." She waited for Sue to follow her instructions. "Now, push the up temperature button until the flashing number reaches four hundred, or four zero zero." Sue pushed the button. "Good, just like that, nicely done."

"So we're ready to put the pizza in?" Sue asked.

"No. You first need to push the start button, so the oven can preheat," Juliana told her. "The oven must heat up to four hundred degrees before we can put the pizzas in. Right now it's not hot."

Sue pushed the start button and stared at the oven, waiting for something to happen.

Denise said, "If you all look in the dark oven, can you see

the glowing red things in the bottom of the oven? Those are the heating elements. They are really hot. Those are what heat up the oven. Don't touch those when the oven is on."

"Now, we can only cook two of these pizzas at one time. So which two should we start with?" Juliana asked the group.

"I'm hungry," replied Tyler.

"Me too," added Zachary. "Can I start?"

Juliana clarified, "Which two *kinds of pizza* should be cooked first?"

"Sausage!" replied the boys in unison.

"Okay, good. And let's bake the cheese pizza too," suggested Juliana. "If everyone wants to try a slice of each kind of pizza, we can do that too."

"I would like to," Martha replied quietly.

"So would I," added Donald.

"Sounds good," said Juliana. "We'll start with the sausage and the cheese pizzas. Let's open these. Sue, can you open the drawer over there... the one on top... that's it, and get the scissors out?"

"These are bigger than the scissors I used to cut pictures with Karen," Sue told the others.

"Yes, scissors can be dangerous. But they're not as dangerous as knives," Juliana added. "We don't want you to use knives yet. That's why we're just using scissors today. Carefully cut the plastic without cutting the pizza or the cardboard that's underneath the pizza." She watched Sue work. "Good."

"Oh! There's the beep from the oven," Denise announced when the oven signaled it was at temperature. "It's now preheated to four hundred degrees. Let's put the pizzas in."

Sue opened the oven door and reached for a rack. "Wow, that's hot!"

"Don't touch that!" Denise cried.

Sue quickly pulled her hands back from the oven rack. She stood up straight, her eyes wide, and took a step back.

"Sorry to scare you Sue," Denise apologized. She put her

hand on Sue's back to calm her. "I thought you were going to touch the racks in the oven."

"I was."

"Please don't," Juliana pleaded. "They're *very* hot. They would burn your hands instantly. You must always use a hot pad or oven gloves."

Denise handed oven mitts to Sue. "These are oven gloves. Put them over your hands. Now you can slide a rack out a bit. Try it." She watched Sue. "Good, like that. Now you can place the pizza on the rack."

"Is that why Emeril Live always uses a towel to get stuff out of the oven, for heat protection? I thought he didn't want to get his hands dirty."

Juliana and Denise laughed. Sue smiled.

The rest of the lesson passed without injury. Denise and Juliana were thankful. Mary was the only one with formal medical training, and she was off for the rest of the day.

The residents ate the pizzas and decided that cheese pizza was boring. They were about equally divided about their preference for the other varieties.

Knowing the residents could not eat pizza for every meal, Denise offered suggestions for dinner and the following morning's breakfast. "Since you had lunch late this afternoon, perhaps a light dinner is in order," she recommended. "You can have peanut butter sandwiches or popcorn this evening. Those are easy to make. Shall we show you how?"

"Ooo! I can make peanut butter and jelly!" Tyler volunteered.

"You can?" asked Denise. "Please tell us how."

"Okay... you take a piece of bread and smear peanut butter on it. And you take another piece of bread and squeeze jelly on it. Then you put the two pieces of bread together... with the stuff on the inside." Tyler's eyes and his smile lit the room with pride.

"Excellent. Can I put you in charge of peanut butter and jelly sandwiches tonight?" Denise asked, sharing his happiness.

"Yeah, sure!""

"Great. Thank you, Tyler."

"What is popcorn?" Donald asked.

"It's corn that has popped inside out," Juliana replied. "It's light and crunchy."

"Is it good?" Donald continued.

"It is if you put butter and salt on it," Denise replied.

"Lots of butter," Juliana added.

"How do you pop it inside out?"

"Heat," Juliana explained. "The little bit of water in the kernel of corn heats, and the water vapor expands. Without any place to go, the kernel explodes. I wish I could show you. It's really cool! I only have microwave popcorn with me. Maybe later I'll get some kernels to show you how it works. No matter how it works, it's good."

"TJ, can you supervise the microwave popcorn?" Denise asked.

"You bet," he replied.

"Thanks."

"Oh!" Juliana added, "Everyone please remember; do not put anything metal in the microwave. Metal reflects the microwaves and overloads the whole thing. It'll ruin it. Please don't do it. Thank you."

"Now, for breakfast tomorrow," Denise continued, "we suggest cereal in milk. We have two kinds for you to choose from. You can have the healthy Raisin Bran, or the sugary sweet Lucky Charms. You just put cereal in a bowl and pour in some milk. Then eat with a spoon. Easy!"

"But remember to keep the milk in the refrigerator," Juliana warned. "Bacteria will grow in it and spoil it in a matter of hours. That's not good. You will know when milk is bad because it will stink."

"We've left bottled water and soda to drink. There should be ice in the freezer," Denise told the residents. "I think that's it for this afternoon. Enjoy your dinner and your evening. We'll see you all tomorrow. If you have an emergency, you can go to the boy's house and get TJ, or you can knock on the door of the Exchange. One of the staff will be there overnight. I think it will be Carl tonight."

"Goodbye everyone," Juliana said.

The others said goodbye to Denise and Juliana as they left Sue's house. The boys and TJ took the opportunity to go back to their cabin to watch TV until dinner.

Martha, Donald, and Sue each got a bottle of water and sat at Sue's kitchen table to talk.

Sue started the conversation by asking both Martha and Donald, "Where did you come from? What happened to you before you came here?"

"Rockford, in Illinois," Martha responded. "My person called the police. They put me in a jail. I was there for many days. They asked questions, but I did not answer. I did not know. Mr. Stevens took me to the hotel. Then we came here."

"What did you do during the day while you were in a jail?" asked Sue.

"Nothing. I sat. I listened to people talk."

"I got to watch TV with my person's girl," Sue volunteered. "And I read books. I learned a lot about animals and the Earth. That's the planet we are on. What about you Donald?"

"I arrived in Florida, behind a store, by a large trash bin. No one noticed me when I arrived," he replied. "When you say 'my person', what do you mean?"

"I look like another person," offered Sue. "The first thing I saw was another person who I look like. Her name is Sue, too. From listening to other people, they think I arrived from her. I heard people mention a substance. One person called it 'goo'."

"Same with me," added Martha. "The first thing I remember was looking at a person. But then she ran away. I looked in a window glass at me and I looked like her. We were the same, except she had on clothes, but I did not. I sat outside with no people until the police took me."

"So do I have a person that looks like me? Do I have another Donald?"

"I don't know," Sue replied. "If the substance or goo that I arrived from with my person is the same for you, then you have a person too. That's why we are all here; because we all arrived from this substance." She paused to let the others think about what she said. Then she asked Donald, "What did you do when you arrived?"

"I sat behind the store. I also did not have any clothes. A nice person from the store gave some to me. She said I looked 'fameeler'. I do not know what that meant, but I put on the clothes. Another man came over to me and we talked. We stayed together for days. We stayed behind the store, out of the sun. It's hot in Florida and you always feel like you're wet. Other people joined us at night. They had carts from the store with stuff in them. They shared food at first. But then one day they asked me to get food. I didn't know how. They said to stand by the store and ask. But the food was inside. So I went inside. Then the police arrived for me. They took me to jail, like Martha. They asked a lot of questions. I could answer some, about the past days. But then they asked where I came from, what I did a long time ago and things like that. I couldn't answer. I didn't know. I was there for two days until Mr. Stevens arrived for me."

"I wonder how the boys arrived here," Sue said aloud. "We'll ask them tonight. Donald, did you read books or watch TV?"

"No. They did not have those behind the store. I had new papers... I think they were called that. They were big pieces of paper with lots of words. They didn't make any sense to me at first, but after talking with other people I started to learn the words. Other people covered themselves at night with the papers. I tried to read them."

"Did you learn anything?"

"I don't think so. The paper mentioned a guy named President a lot. And there were a lot of words about money and people not having jobs. But I didn't understand what it all meant."

"We have a TV here," noted Sue. "Let's turn it on and see what's on."

They moved into the sitting room in Sue's house where the TV was located. She turned it on and started flipping between the few available channels.

"Ooo! SpongeBob! This is one of my favorites." Sue sang the theme song, "Sponge Bob Square Pants, Sponge Baaaaaaahb, Square Pants!"

The three adults sat and watched cartoons.

The boys and TJ arrived at Sue's around dusk and joined the adults in watching TV. When it was completely dark outside, TJ asked if anyone was hungry. The others nodded. Tyler asked who would like peanut butter sandwiches. He was excited to show everyone what he could do. Each agreed to have a sandwich. TJ also offered to make popcorn.

"I want to see how popcorn pops itself inside out," Donald said eagerly.

"Unfortunately, Donald, you can't see it with microwave popcorn. You can't open the bag while it's popping or you won't have enough heat to pop the corn."

"It pops in a bag? How does the corn get in the bag?"

"They make it that way. You put the bag in the microwave and pop it. Then you open it and eat. Here, let me show you." He led the others into the kitchen.

TJ removed the plastic wrapper from a bag of the popcorn and placed the bag in the microwave. The residents followed his every move to see how the corn popped. He started the microwave and everyone stared at the bag rotating inside. At the first pop they all jumped. They watched, wide-eyed, as the bag expanded from the popping kernals. When the microwave stopped, TJ opened the door and the sweet smell rolled over the residents. Silently, they drooled as they watched TJ open the bag and dump the contents in a bowl. They dug in and started munching the buttery kernels.

"So the inside of popcorn is yellow and smells this good? Wow. I like it!" Donald exclaimed.

"Actually, popcorn is white when it pops," TJ clarified. "This kind that you're eating is flavored with butter. That's what makes it yellow and taste really good."

"I *like* butter," Donald said.

"We all do, Donald," TJ said with a smile. "So, now that we've had our popcorn, should Tyler make us all PB and J's?"

The five residents gave him a look of confusion.

"PB and J's... you know... peanut butter and jelly sandwiches."

The collective "Oh," from the group indicated they got it.

Tyler made sandwiches for all. He carefully spread the peanut butter and the jelly, and he cut the sandwiches diagonally. He smiled the whole time.

Everyone received a sandwich and sat around the table, eating and talking. They found it difficult to sustain conversation because of the need to drink something to un-stick the peanut butter from their mouths. But the residents all enjoyed the new taste and texture sensation.

After they cleaned up, Sue started a conversation with the boys. "Tyler, you came from Maryland. That's a state by Washington DC, our capitol." She looked at the others and said, "I learned that from a book I read at Karen's house."

"Yeah, Maryland," Tyler responded. "I stayed with Billy Philips. He's nice. He looks like me. His mom called us twins. She didn't like me. But I liked Billy. We watched TV and played video games. Billy wanted to play outside, but his mom wouldn't let me go out. She said she didn't want anyone to see me."

"How long were you there?" asked Sue.

"I forgot. I think it was like four days... maybe five."

"And then Mr. Stevens took you to the hotel?"

TJ looked at Sue with concern. *How did she know that? She couldn't know that, could she?*

Sue noticed TJ and responded to him, "Each of the adults was picked up and moved here by Mr. Stevens. I guessed that the boys were also picked up and moved by Mr. Stevens."

"Yeah, Mr. Stevens came and got me," Tyler answered. "Now I don't have Billy to play with."

"And you Zachary? Where did you come from?" Sue continued.

TJ squirmed in his chair, although no one noticed. He wondered if Ted would let the conversation continue. After a little thought, he guessed that if they knew about four of the five residents, it couldn't hurt to find out about the last.

"A place called peegrum that was close to nayshvill. In tensee," said Zachary.

"Is that how you say the name of that state? Karen's state book said it was ten-is-see, and the city is nash-ville."

"Y'all may say that. But the people called it 'nayshvil'."

"Okay, 'nayshvil' it is," Sue responded. "What did you do there?" she asked Zachary.

"They kept me in the dark," he began, "in their ter-nader cellar. I ate meals with the people... the lady said it wasn't right to eat in the dark. But they kept me alone the rest of the time. A man... I think they called him sherf... came and looked at me a few times. He said it was too weird that I looked like the other Zachary. He told the others that he called the dee-aych-ess but didn't know when they would get there. Then Mr. Stevens arrived and took me to the hotel and then here."

"Thank you for telling us where you arrived," Sue said. "I'm from Kansas. I lived with the other Sue and her girl Karen. She was really nice. Karen and I are like sisters. And Martha is from Illinois and Donald is from Florida."

Hoping to keep the information sharing to a minimum, TJ stood and suggested that it was late and everyone should return to their house and go to sleep.

"But I didn't get to watch my movie," protested Donald.

"You have all day tomorrow to watch it," TJ replied. "And you can go to the Exchange and get more movies. You can do all that and more tomorrow. I think we should all go to bed now."

Everyone agreed, Donald somewhat reluctantly. They left Sue alone in her house.

She went into her bedroom and pulled back the white sheets. She climbed into bed and tried to get comfortable. Her new clothes kept poking her around the waist. And her shirt twisted around her as she tried to get comfortable. She finally remembered what Mary told her about what to wear at night. She got out of bed and found the pile of clothes she received. She picked up the long t-shirt and looked at it before taking off the shorts and shirt she was wearing. She put the night shirt on, admired it a bit, and then climbed back into bed. She smiled as she got comfortable, and quickly fell asleep.

Chapter 20 - Free Lunch

Everyone at the laboratory was assembled in the front conference room. It was a tight squeeze. But no one was going to miss a free lunch. Dr. Bailey knew this would lift morale, but he also knew, being a Friday, little work would get done in the afternoon.

The group cheered when the catering van pulled up to the front door. Dr. Bailey tried to keep control of the crowd long enough to let the caterer bring in the food and set up. Behind the first cart of sandwiches, Mr. Stevens walked in the front door. Only Dr. Bailey noticed the visitor. He walked up to Ted and they shook hands.

"Hi Jim. Word on the street is there's free food," Ted said with a smile. "Who's the sucker that sprung for the spread? I want to get in on it."

"Then you better get in the scrum," Jim told him. "There won't be anything left in about five minutes. They're like a pack of hyenas. But they will certainly enjoy and appreciate it. Thank you."

"*You* better get in there, Jim," Ted said, pointing to the food.

"Ah, I'll scavenge for a few scraps after they're finished," Jim replied.

"When the frenzy is over, can I have a word with you and your group leaders?" Ted asked.

"Sure. We have some new findings to share with you that I think you'll find interesting."

"You have new findings since Monday? You people *do* work fast."

The two men stood against the wall in a corner of the conference room and observed the analysts devour and enjoy the free lunch.

The din of the frenzy faded after forty minutes and the analysts gradually returned to the labs. Dr. Bailey asked the group leaders to get their data and return to the conference room to talk with Mr. Stevens.

Jim and Ted were able to find enough fixings to make a couple sandwiches. And there were even a couple cans of soda remaining. *Amazing!* They ate as the caterer cleaned up and headed out. Shortly after, the group leaders came back to the conference room.

"So, Ted, you wanted a word with us?" Jim asked when his group leaders took seats.

"No, no," Ted replied, shaking his head. He smiled and said, "You have new data. That's much better. Let's start with the new results."

"You're on, Cindy," Jim told her.

Brimming with excitement, Cindy started downloading data. "I analyzed the substance from the pod in the meteorite. I hydrolyzed the membrane proteins... chewed them to individual pieces with acid, to do some elemental analysis. The amino acid content was off the chart. These are some seriously huge proteins. And I found nucleic acids! We didn't detect any before because we weren't looking for them. We were correct earlier... uh... this week, right?"

"Yes, just four days ago," Ted answered.

"These proteins are super densely-packed... denser than natural proteins, and they have a lot of genetic material imbedded, way more than I expected," Cindy said. "I don't think our best biochemical or analytical techniques will be able to separate any intact genetic material from the membrane proteins. I don't think we'll be able to do any sequencing of either the DNA or the proteins."

"Even if we could separate the DNA, there's way too much stuff," Sarah added. "We'd never make a dent to sequence it if we tried, not for a hundred years."

"Yeah, how long did it take to sequence the human genome? And they had lots of labs working on it," Bruno pointed out.

"Are you saying there's an entire alien genome in these proteins?" Ted asked.

"I don't know if it's an entire genome," Jim replied. "But there are a lot of nucleotides."

"I don't think we can identify a genetic message. The best we can say is there's a lot of stuff in that goo," Cindy clarified.

"Tell me, what does all that stuff do?"

"Other than transform, or clone animals, we don't know, Ted. And we won't know specifically what it all does, at least not anytime soon," Jim replied.

After a moment of silence to ponder the new information, Mr. Stevens snapped to attention and began a new subject. "I'd like you all to put your astrophysicist hats on. If you don't have an astrophysicist hat, put on your general science hats and let's do some more postulating. I want to know where this stuff came from.

"You mean, from where in space?" Jim asked for clarification.

"Yes. Where did the pods originate?"

"We don't know," Bruno replied.

"Duh, Bruno," Sarah snapped. "He asked us to postulate."

"The pods were sent to Earth. Were they dropped off? Were they launched?" Ted asked.

Jim reminded him, "Didn't we conclude earlier that they weren't dropped off, because if an alien species had traveled here, why would they drop off goo that increases the local population? Why not travel the rest of the distance to Earth and take over, right?"

"So this was a passive delivery?" Ted asked.

"It makes more sense," Bruno thought out loud.

"Then these pods were launched to Earth. From where?"

"From a long way away," Jim replied.

The group leaders chuckled. Their boss' response sounded so simple, but it was true; the goo was sent from a very long way away.

"How far?" Ted asked.

"If they were sent from somewhere in our galaxy, they travelled... let me Google it, hold on," Jim said. "Milky Way diameter... um... here it is... one hundred thousand light years."

"How far is a light year?" Cindy wondered.

"I gotta Google that too. Light year... light year... let's see... a light year is... five point eight seven trillion miles. Wow! You really can find everything on the internet, can't you?"

"So we're talking... what... six hundred quadrillion miles to get across the galaxy?" Ted asked. "Now that's a road trip."

Cindy pointed out, "There's no way these pods could get here in our lifetime, as in, not in *human beings'* lifetime."

"How the hell fast would these have to travel?" Sarah asked.

"It all depends on when they were sent," Jim answered. "If they were sent five billion years ago, when our solar system formed... we're talking... hold on... let me calculate it... uh... around thirteen thousand miles an hour. That's slower than what it takes to escape Earth's orbit. They would certainly have to launch pods faster than that."

"What if they could launch them at a hundred thousand miles an hour?" Ted wondered. "That's about seven times faster. When would they have been launched?"

"Hold on, let me calculate... um... Six hundred seventy

million years ago."

Ted scribbled on his note pad, and then responded, "At a million miles an hour, that's seven hundred times slower than the speed of light, the pods would have been launched when dinosaurs went extinct."

They all paused to consider Mr. Steven's comment.

"Can you launch something at a million miles an hour?" Bruno asked.

No one knew. They all shook their heads and shrugged.

"What if the pods came from another galaxy?" Ted wondered.

"The closest galaxy is hundreds of millions of light years away," Jim replied. "They'd be travelling for... I don't know... billions of years? At some point, unless pods travel at the speed of light, there are places in the universe from which a pod could not possibly reach us. The pods would have to have been launched before the universe was formed."

"So...?" Ted asked.

"So..." Jim deduced, "if we assume normal physics, I'd guess the pods were sent from within our own galaxy. Depending on how fast and when they were launched, the aliens could be relatively close, or they could be on the opposite side of the galaxy. There's no way to know."

Chapter 21 – The Way Things Are

As they had done the past several days, the adults met at Sue's house in the morning for breakfast. Sue had mastered coffee, toast, and was getting better at scrambled eggs. Cereal, specifically Fruit Loops--their favorite, was always an option for breakfast, but Martha and Donald were willing to try Sue's new culinary creations.

Sue had her white towel thrown over her shoulder as she scrambled eggs.

"Did you use butter in the pan?" Donald inquired. "That makes it so much better. Butter makes everything better. And yesterday you forgot something in the eggs. They didn't taste right."

"Yes, I used butter, Donald. And I know I forgot salt in the eggs yesterday. But I'm still learning. I'm mostly trying to keep from burning myself on the stove. 'Safety first,' that's what Mary always says."

She pulled the towel off her shoulder to hold the handle of the pan as she moved it over to the plates on the counter. She plated the eggs and added slices of toast to each. She delivered the plates to her guests. "Here you go. Toast with strawberry jam, scrambled eggs, and coffee."

"Denise told me about cream in coffee. Do you have any

cream?" Martha asked.

"Juliana gave me half and half, but said it was the same as cream." Sue went to the refrigerator and took out the carton. "Here, try this."

Martha added some to her coffee. "Mmmm... Denise was right. Coffee is better with cream. Try it Donald."

"No thanks, Martha. I like it plain."

"It might be as good as butter is on toast," Sue suggested.

"Okay, I'll try it." He had a sip from Martha's cup. "It's okay, but I think I like it better plain."

The three sat and enjoyed the food Sue had prepared. Martha especially liked the coffee.

Donald looked outside and asked, "Have you noticed how there have been more trucks driving around? And they're fixing four more houses. Do you think we're getting more residents in our community?"

"I hope so," Sue replied, raising her eyebrows. "I like meeting new people."

"So do I," added Martha. "Before I got here I never met anyone... well... anyone I liked."

Donald frowned and said, "The new people better not try to change things. I like the way things are now."

"Why would they?" Sue wondered. "When we arrived here, we didn't know anything and all started together. But now we've been here for many days so we know a lot more than they do. We'll help them and they'll learn how we do things."

"But what if they know more than we do?" Donald asked nervously. "You know a lot, Sue, because you read a lot of books. But not all of us know as much as you. I haven't read a lot of books. What if the new people have read more books than you? They'll try to tell us how to do things."

"They might, Donald, or they'll learn how to live here with us and we'll help them. And the more they know, the more we'll learn. I think it will be good to have new residents," Sue said confidently.

"I hope you're right."

After breakfast, followed by an hour of watching cooking shows on the Food Network, the adults returned to their respective houses to get dressed. Ten minutes later they met on Main Street, across from the entrance to the Exchange.

They each had dirty clothes in laundry bags. Donald had a DVD, and Sue had a book to exchange.

After greeting Denise and Blake, and exchanging clothes, dirty for clean, the residents went to the entertainment section. Sue, Martha, and Denise looked at books while Donald and Blake discussed the last movie Donald watched. "If the wizard was all-powerful, why did he come out from behind the curtain?" Donald asked, confused. "Why didn't he grant everyone's wishes after they brought the witch's broom?"

Laughing politely, Blake answered, "Well... he wasn't really an all-powerful wizard. He was a fake wizard."

"Fake wizard? Why did the people of Oz believe he was real? Why did they let him be the wizard?"

"I'm not sure. I think he tricked them into believing he was a wizard. And once he had the big head and fire, no one challenged him."

"So the whole time Dorothy looked for a guy who was a fake?" Donald asked, even more confused.

"Remember, it was all a dream."

"It was?" Donald asked. "Really?" He shook his head and sighed.

Blake laughed again. "Remember the black and white part of the film, at the beginning and the end of the movie?"

"Yeah," Donald replied.

"That was the real part. The color part of the movie was Dorothy's dream."

"I just don't get it." Donald threw his hands up in the air. "Do you have a movie that is... all real?"

Blake smiled and put his hand on Donald's shoulder. He understood Donald's frustration. "Let's take a look at each of these to see if we can find one you'd like." Blake sat with Donald and attempted to find a movie that Donald might understand and enjoy.

Meanwhile, Sue and Martha looked for books. "I like the books about animals and the states. I read a few stories at Karen's, like Jamberry and Sheep in a Jeep. They were silly. They were good stories, but not a lot of information. I liked reading all of Karen's books about Earth and animals and stuff."

"So I should find books about animals?" Martha asked.

"Sure, unless you want to read silly stories instead. I'll help you read either kind," Sue offered.

"Maybe we should read both kinds."

"Okay. Let's start with the Big Book of Animals and Good Night Moon. That will help you practice reading." Turning to Denise, Sue asked, "Do you have books about the states? I read another book about the fifty states. I want to read more."

"We have a few of these 'Everything' books," Denise replied. "Everything Kids Nature... Everything Kids Geography... and yes, here we go, Everything Kids States."

"Can I read all of them?" Sue inquired.

"Yeah, I guess so," Denise replied, shrugging her shoulders.

"Good. Now, what about more food ideas for me to cook? I want to learn to make more food. Everyone liked spa... spag--"

"Spaghetti. I'm glad they liked it," Denise said.

"So what else can I make?"

"How about hamburgers?" Denise suggested. "Would you like to try hamburgers?"

"Maybe, but I didn't like the stuff I had on it at Karen's house. It was too... I don't know... sweet, I think." She scrunched her nose and closed her eyes while shaking her head. "I don't think I'll like it again."

"You know you can change the stuff you put on hamburgers, right?"

"You can?" Sue was surprised, but happy to know she had options.

Denise replied, "Yeah, sure. You can put many different things on burgers. The number of possibilities is endless! You can put just about anything on a burger."

"What do most people like? What do you like?"

"Most people like ketchup and mustard. The ketchup was probably what you thought was sweet. Maybe you don't like ketchup. People also like mayonnaise, spicy brown mustard, pickle relish, onions, bacon, cheese, barbecue sauce, and salsa."

"Can we try them all?" Sue asked.

"Not all at once," Denise replied, laughing. "You could eat hamburgers for a week and not try all the combinations. I suggest eating sliders."

Sue frowned. "I thought we're going to have hamburgers."

"Sliders are small hamburgers," Denise replied with a smile. "If you have small burgers, you can have two or three and have different toppings on each. You can find out which toppings you like best."

"Cool!" Sue's frown gave way to a smile. "Let's make sliders tonight!"

"Do you have coffee here?" Martha interrupted.

Denise was startled by the sudden change of subject. "Uh... no, we don't have a coffee maker here in the Exchange."

"She really likes coffee," Sue told Denise.

"You should get a coffee maker here," Martha recommended. "So we can read books here and drink coffee."

"Oh, like Barnes and Nobles," Denise said.

"Who?" asked Sue.

"It's a book store. They serve coffee and pastries in the store. People sit in the stores to read and drink coffee. I guess they buy books too, otherwise they wouldn't do it."

"Why not?"

"Businesses only do things that make money. If they lose money, they go out of business... they close. So, having coffee and allowing the shoppers to read in the store must result in more book sales than if they didn't have coffee and allow shoppers to read in the store."

"We should have coffee here," Martha insisted.

"We'll see what we can do," Denise told her with a smile.

"Thanks."

Denise turned to Sue, "Shall we go look for burger toppings?"

"And something else to go with the burgers," Sue added.

Sue, Martha, and Denise moved to the food section. They invited Donald to join them. They selected a few bottles of condiments and looked over the available chips. They chose tortilla chips and salsa to accompany the burgers. Denise gave Sue two pounds of ground beef and told her how to portion, season and cook the hamburgers.

"Would you like me to come over tonight?" Denise offered.

"Sure, but only if you want to *eat* burgers. I think I can cook them myself. I'd like to try. I hope the others are as excited as I am to eat burgers."

"I'm sure they are," Denise told Sue. Donald and Martha nodded in agreement. "I think they like it that you're the cook. And you're good at it. I'll let you cook by yourself tonight."

Chapter 22 - New Arrivals

The next morning, as usual, Donald and Martha arrived at Sue's house for breakfast. Sue had coffee ready and waiting.

"Thank you, Sue," Martha told her. "I'm so glad you know how to make coffee."

Sue wasn't sure, but she had begun to detect a little grouch in Martha before she got her coffee. Wanting to avoid that grouch, Sue made sure a fresh cup was on the table each morning, waiting for Martha. "Cream?" she offered.

"Please. Thank you, Sue." Martha took her first sip. "Aah, good coffee."

"Cream for your coffee, Donald?" Sue asked.

"No thanks," he replied.

Someone knocked on the door. They all turned to see Denise standing at the door. Sue's eyes lit up. So did Donald's.

"Denise!" Sue called as she let her guest in. "Why are you here so early?"

"I wanted to give you a new breakfast idea before you started this morning."

"A new idea? Thanks! What is it?"

"Pancakes, you'll love 'em. By the way, how did burgers go last night?"

"Great!" Sue replied

"They were delicious," Donald chimed in.

"What toppings did you all have?" Denise asked.

"I had ketchup and mustard and onions and cheese on one. And I had pickles and mayonnaise and mustard on the other," Donald said. They were both really good."

"I tried ketchup on one bite of mine," Sue told Denise. "You were right. It was the ketchup that made it sweet. I didn't like it." She made the same face she had the day before. "So I had mustard and onions and cheese on one. And I had mustard and pickles on the other. Oh! And I like salsa too! I like the medium kind. It makes my mouth hot. What makes the food that way?"

"There are hot peppers that make things spicy. It seems like you like spicy food," Denise said.

"I do."

"And you, Martha, what toppings did you have on your burgers?"

"I had B B Q sauce and cheese on one, and ketchup and cheese on the other. They were good. Sue makes really good burgers... and good coffee."

"You love your coffee, don't you Martha?" Denise laughed. Martha smiled. "Shall we get started on the pancakes?"

Donald and Martha sat back while Denise showed Sue how to make pancakes. Sue asked a lot of questions while they cooked to make sure she understood the instructions on the box. She wanted to re-create pancakes again when Denise was not there to help.

After eating a big stack of pancakes, all four sat back in their chairs and sipped coffee.

"Denise, that was the best breakfast yet," Donald complimented.

"Uh... Hello! I helped!" Sue protested.

"Sorry. Good idea, Denise, and good cooking, Sue."

"Thank you," Sue responded. She nodded at Donald.

Donald turned to Denise. "We've noticed a lot more trucks around here. It looks like they've fixed up four more houses. Are we getting new residents?"

"It was supposed to be a secret," Denise answered. "But it's hard to keep one when you guys see all the activity. But I can tell you now. Yes, we have more residents arriving. They arrive today."

"More people?" asked Martha.

"Same as us," Sue answered.

Looking concerned, Denise asked Sue, "In what way?"

"Well... you know... people who have copies, people who have others that look like them, people who came from the substance."

Denise hid her expression well. She was shocked that Sue knew so much about the nature of their origin.

"I want to talk with them to see where they came from," Sue said. "I'm interested in meeting the new people."

"This will be weird," Donald added. "We've been here for a while. They'll be new. How will they fit in?"

"We have not been here for that long," Martha said. "We can add new people. We can teach them in the same way Sue teaches us."

"I agree," Sue concluded. "We can all change a little to bring new people into our community. It's not like we've lived here all our lives."

"No," Donald acknowledged, "but we've lived half our lives here." Suddenly, he remembered, "Hey, we've never named our town. Mr. Stevens said we could name this town. What should it be?"

"Independent," Sue immediately replied. "Our town should be called Independent, U.S.A., because we live the way we want. We're independent. I got that from a book I read."

Donald and Martha nodded in agreement.

Looking at the clock on the microwave, Denise stood up and told the others, "Mr. Stevens asked if you all can meet the new residents at the Exchange at nine o'clock. That's in about twenty minutes. Can you do that?"

Each agreed.

Denise walked to the door. She too had to get to the Exchange. As she opened the door to leave, Donald told her, "Thanks again, Denise, for giving us a new breakfast."

"You are all welcome," she replied. "We'll see you soon. Don't be late." Denise left to go to the Exchange.

Donald and Martha sipped coffee for a few minutes, and then returned to their houses to change out of their pajamas. Sue changed her clothes and watched the end of the show on Food Network. The three met, as usual, on Main Street and walked across the street to the Exchange. As they crossed the street, a jet landed on the air field.

"There they are," Donald announced.

"Let's wait inside," Sue suggested.

The adult residents were joined by the boys inside the Exchange. They looked around to see what might be of interest today. But no one looked seriously. They were stalling, waiting for the new residents to arrive.

A white van pulled up to the building. Three girls and three adults climbed out of the van, as did three new staff members, dressed in khaki shorts and blue shirts. Mr. Stevens emerged from the front passenger seat and escorted the new residents into the Exchange. Sue and the others came to the front for the introductions.

"Good morning," Ted called out. "I'd like to first introduce the new residents to this community and then I'll introduce the other residents, the counselors, and the Exchange employees.

"Ladies first... this is Kati, she's age six."

Kati was scared, as expected for such a young person. She tried to stay close to the other girls. No one could see her bright blue eyes. All anyone saw was her blonde hair as she tried to hide her face.

"This is Violet, she's seven," Ted continued.

Violet was much less scared than Kati. She was shy, but

only because she was meeting many new people at once. She looked at each person with her hazel eyes. She smiled timidly. She was about six inches taller than Kati. Her long blonde hair was pulled back in a pony tail.

"And this is Brandy, she's thirteen."

Brandy was wearing the latest fashions for young women. She dressed older than she actually was. Juliana and Denise took notice of her clothes and were jealous. Brandy hid her face behind her long black hair. She looked defiantly through squinted eyes at each person. She was trying to decide which of them could be trusted.

"We also have Patsy joining us," Ted continued.

Patsy appeared to be around twenty. She wore a t-shirt and jeans. She was tall and fit. She looked like she might play soccer or volleyball. She was not shy, nor skeptical, like the other girls. She waved and said, "Hi!" to each new person she met.

"And last, but not least, we have Janet and Larry."

Janet was middle-aged, as was Larry. They were both five and a half feet tall. They were not fat, but not skinny. Janet had short styled brown hair. She was wearing a print shirt and matching shorts. Larry had black hair under his Pioneer Hi-Bred Seed hat. He had on a white t-shirt, overalls, and work boots. They both smiled at the others as they were introduced.

Walking over to Sue and the others, Ted continued the introductions. "These two young men are Tyler and Zachary. And these three residents are Martha, Donald, and Sue. They can each show you where they live and can help you get settled. I invite you new residents to ask these old timers for assistance." He smiled at Sue. "As for the staff here, we have Mary, Juliana, Denise, and Carl. They work here at the Exchange. They can take care of all your needs. The boy's counselors are Blake, TJ, and Cody. And you girls know the counselors who traveled with you: Heather, Courtney, and Hannah."

Like the boys' counselors, Heather, Courtney, and

Hannah were mirror images of each other. They too looked out of place in their uniforms. They should have been walking advertisements for Aeropostale or Abercrombie & Finch. They had long styled hair, but wore little make-up. Ted wouldn't allow it.

Ted spread his arms wide and announced, "Welcome to all," indicating that introductions were over. "I'll ask Mary and Carl to escort the new arrivals over to the table by the side wall. We have some safety tips to go over with you. And Carl is going to collect some information from you. The rest of you can shop and wait for the others."

As the group dispersed, Denise asked to have a word with Mr. Stevens. She pointed to a spot away from the others and walked with him. "A few things for you, Ted. First, the residents would like some chairs to sit in here at the Exchange to read books... you know...a change of scenery from their houses. And they'd like to have a coffee maker."

"Like a book store," Ted said.

"Exactly."

"I think we can arrange for that. There's no harm in providing a little convenience, a place to sit and read. We have enough folding chairs for now. I'll look into something more comfortable. And, sure, we can order a coffee maker for here in the Exchange."

"Second," Denise continued, "I was at breakfast with Sue and the others this morning. They figured out new residents were arriving. That wasn't difficult. But that's not the surprise. Sue knew where she came from. Not the location, but how she came to be. She knew about the substance. She knows she's a copy of another person."

"I knew this would happen at some point," Ted admitted. "Though, it's a lot earlier than I would have wanted. Sue is smart, and was not isolated like the others. So she had a lot of exposure to the real world. Knowledge of her existence is not an issue as long as she stays contained here at the base. That goes for them all."

"But if they keep learning, they can't stay here forever."

"We'll monitor how they progress," he reassured her. "The most important thing is to make sure they don't do anything crazy. The general public can't know about them."

"And lastly," Denise continued, "I think they've selected a name for their town... Independent, U.S.A."

"How ironic," Ted responded flatly.

"I thought you'd want to know."

"Thank you very much, Denise." He tapped her arm a couple times and smiled. "I'm glad I can rely on you and the others to keep things in order. I appreciate everything you do."

Denise smiled back at Ted and returned to the group.

Ted moved to the entrance of the Exchange and announced to all, "I must leave for my next appointment. I welcome the new residents and the new counselors, and bid farewell to you all. Have a good day."

Ted exited the Exchange, climbed in the passenger seat of the van and was driven back to the jet waiting at the air field.

"I can cook for everyone, but I can't fit them all in my house," Sue said. "Where can we all eat?"

Denise and Juliana talked with Sue in the food section of the Exchange, helping her plan the evening meal. "I think we have enough tables and chairs for everyone here in the Exchange," Juliana replied. "So I think we can set up in the open space behind the shelves. We might need to borrow dishes from each house. Or are they all in your house, Sue, since everyone eats with you?"

"I have dishes from Martha and Donald, but not from the new residents."

"Okay, we'll make sure we get enough dishes. We can cook in your kitchen, correct? It's the closest house to the Exchange. We can bring the hot food across the street.

How does that sound?" Juliana asked.

"That sounds good," Sue replied. "Now, what are we going to cook? Spaghetti is getting old. I want to try something new. I saw Bobby Flay cook fried chicken on TV. Can we do that?"

"I think we have some frozen chicken," Juliana said. "But we have to take it out now to let it thaw."

"I'll get it," Denise offered. She walked over to the freezer.

"I don't think we can do fried chicken cooked in oil," Juliana told Sue. "That will be a big mess and will be a fire hazard. We would have to cook for a long time to make enough for everyone. But we can make Shake-and-Bake chicken. It has a breading on it, but you bake the chicken in the oven. So it's safe and we can cook all of it at the same time."

"Good. That sounds good. Can we also have grits?" Sue asked.

"I don't think we have grits. But we do have potatoes. We can have mashed potatoes," Juliana offered. "Will that work?"

"Potatoes... yeah, let's make mashed potatoes with... um... garlic... and cheese!"

"Was that one of Emeril's dishes?" Denise asked, as she returned with the frozen chicken.

"No. It's one of my dishes. Well... I've never tried it, but garlic and potatoes and cheese together sounds really good. Do you think it will taste good?"

"Yeah, I do," Denise replied. "I think it will taste really good."

"That sounds great," Juliana said. "Can we assist you? Can we be your sous chefs, Sue?"

Smiling and giggling, she pretended to be a cranky head chef. "Sure, but don't slow me down. And you better jump when I say jump or I'll fire you!"

"Let's get shopping... er... May we start shopping, Chef?" Denise asked.

"Yes. Start shopping," Sue instructed. The three women smiled at each other and laughed as they started shopping.

Patsy, Janet, Larry, and the girls returned from their orientation and joined Donald and Martha in the book and DVD section. Donald took the lead to describe the movies to the new residents, being careful not to give away the plot or the ending for those he had already seen. Martha shared her ideas about the best books, those that she had read with Sue.

Carl and Mary set up chairs toward the back of the exchange. Mary then called to everyone to sit. As they all took seats on the folding chairs, Martha said, "We need coffee."

"Mr. Stevens said he'd look into ordering a coffee maker, Martha," Denise informed her.

"He did? Good. Thank you."

Not wasting any time, Sue began the conversation with the new residents. "Hi! My name is Sue. I came from Kansas. I like to cook and read books and watch the Food Network. Everyone lets me cook. Hi Patsy, can you tell us about you? Where did you come from?"

Startled by Sue's direct questioning, Patsy stuttered, "I... uh... I... I came from Saint Louis."

"That's in Missouri. What did you do in St Louis?"

"I lived with Dana... the person I look like. She's in college."

"How long did you live with her?" Sue asked.

"About a week. I... uh... appeared on a Friday night."

"And?" Sue asked, digging for more information. "How did you appear?"

Carl and Mary looked to each other, concerned. Denise saw their reaction and, recalling her conversation with Ted, slowly held up her hand.

Patsy answered Sue, "There was a party in, like, a park or a forest. When I came out from behind a tree, everyone was laughing at me. They thought I had left my clothes somewhere. Dana, my other me, was in the forest with a boy. When she saw me and the way everyone was laughing, she freaked out. She ran over to me and told everyone that my name was Patsy and I was her cousin. Then she ran me back to her dorm room and gave me clothes to wear."

Not at all surprised by Patsy's answer, Sue continued, "What did you do during the week?"

"I stayed in the room. Dana went to classes. A few of her friends came to visit. They listened to music and studied in the room. We talked a lot. They told me all about them and about college. Dana brought food to me. Then a man came to the room with Dana. I think he was like a professor or something. She looked really nervous, like she was scared. He didn't say much. He, like, looked from me to her, and then said he'd call someone."

"And then Mr. Stevens arrived?" Sue asked.

"Yeah, a couple days later. How'd you know?"

"I guessed," Sue told her.

Denise tried to take control of the conversation. She asked, "Brandy, will you tell us something about yourself?"

"Um... my name is Brandy. I lived in New York. Not the city, but in the middle of the state... Ithaca, New York."

Sue jumped in, "How long did you live there?"

"Four or five days, I think. The parents of Brandy didn't like me. They called the police who came to the house. Then Mr. Stevens brought me here."

"Did you go to school?" Sue asked.

"No, they left me at their house during the day. I watched TV and played video games and surfed the internet. I listened to music and talked with Brandy at night. She was cool, but her parents kinda sucked."

Taking a cue from Denise, Mary tried to include everyone in the conversation, so as not to go too deep into anyone's history. "Kati, can you tell us where you lived before moving here, to you new home?"

Kati didn't respond. She was too scared.

Sue tried to help. She bent down low to try to see Kati's face and quietly said, "Hi Kati. My name is Sue. I like to watch SpongeBob SquarePants. Have you watched SpongeBob?"

"Yes. I... I have," she quietly replied.

"Do you like it?"

"Yes, I do."

"I like it too," Violet added. "It's really funny."

Sue continued making the girls more comfortable. "Patrick is my favorite because he's so dumb. And of course I like SpongeBob."

"Me too," Violet agreed.

"I like SpongeBob. But I didn't see him a lot," Kati said softly. "I only saw one show."

Mary looked at Sue, Kati, and Violet and asked them, "While you three ladies discuss SpongeBob, may I ask the other residents a couple questions?"

Sue nodded with a smile.

Turning to Janet, Mary asked, "Janet, can you tell us about you?"

"I came from Wisconsin," she replied.

"So did I," Larry added. "Mr. Stevens picked us up together."

"Yah. I came from Verona," Janet said.

"And I came from Monroe."

Juliana chimed in, "Cheeseheads, ay? I was born and raised in Minnesota. Good thing it's summer. You probably wouldn't have liked it there in winter. They get feet of snow. And it's really cold."

"Snow? What's snow?" Donald asked.

"It's rain that has frozen in the atmosphere," Juliana told him. "Snow is little ice flakes, they call them snowflakes, that fall in the winter when the temperature is close to or below freezing."

"How cold is freezing?" asked Sue, not wanting to be left out of any conversation.

"It's thirty two degrees Fahrenheit," Juliana replied. "That's the temperature at which water freezes."

"Like ice cubes in a freezer?" Sue wondered.

"A household freezer is actually colder," Juliana said. "It freezes things to about five degrees."

"How hot is it here? Is it hotter than freezing?" Donald asked.

"Yes," Juliana replied with a chuckle. "Much hotter. It's ninety degrees outside."

"Is that normal? Is it always ninety degrees outside?" Sue asked.

"No," Juliana said. "In the summer it's hot and in the winter it's colder. Where we are, it's warmer than Wisconsin, especially in the winter."

Mary interrupted to redirect the conversation. "Janet, Larry... what did you do in Wisconsin?"

"I worked on the farm with the other Larry. He said that as long as I was there I should help him. So I did. He had dairy cows. But the local sheriff heard about me. He came one day and looked at me. He wanted to take me to... I don't know where he wanted to take me, but Larry wouldn't let him. He said I was a good worker. And he said I didn't cost nuthin'."

"I stayed at the house," Janet replied. "The other Janet called the sheriff right away. He said I must stay at the house and not go anywhere. I was only there one night. Mr. Stevens came the next day. Larry was with him. We drove to the airplane and then we came here."

Carl decided enough information had been shared and cut off discussion. He suggested, "Why don't we get some new clothes and some food for our new residents?"

"They don't need food," Sue corrected. "I'll cook for them. I want to." She smiled with pride.

"Okay, we'll get them other supplies and get them settled in their houses," Carl said.

Patsy, Janet, and Larry stood up with Carl and Mary. They walked to the shelves to get supplies. The counselors followed Carl and Mary, as did Kati, Violet and Brandy. Donald also stood up and walked to the shelves. He decided to wait for the others in the DVD section to give advice, in case it was wanted.

Denise and Juliana remained seated with Sue and Martha, discussing logistics for dinner that night. "I suggest we coat the chicken first, and then clean the potatoes for boiling," Denise offered. "Do you agree, Chef?"

"I do," replied Sue. "We also need to make sure we have the garlic and cheese and butter and milk ready for the potatoes."

"And we have to make sure we have coffee," Martha reminded the others.

"You and your coffee, Martha," Juliana responded. "Of course, we'll have coffee for you."

"When should we start cooking?" Sue asked.

"It's not even lunch time," Denise said. "We don't need to start cooking dinner until five o'clock or so. We need to arrange for lunch first. Let's go find some stuff for sandwiches."

As promised, Juliana and Denise arrived at Sue's house promptly at 5:00. Sue gave Denise the task of making sure all the guests would be assembled in the Exchange and the table set on time. Sue volunteered Donald to help Denise. Juliana agreed to assist with cooking dinner. Martha was in charge of the after-dinner coffee. Juliana asked Sue if she could assist with that as well.

After Chef Sue made her assignments, she reviewed the menu. "Okay, we need to make my garlic cheesy mashed potatoes and the bake and shake chicken. We also need the salad."

"Um... chef," Juliana interrupted, "it's shake and bake, not 'bake and shake'."

"Well, I can't be bothered with the name," she said, waving her hand, dismissing the technicality. "Let's get cooking," she announced, determined to start preparing the meal. "Which takes longer, the chicken or the potatoes?

The chicken I think. Where's the box with the instructions?"

Juliana and Martha assisted as instructed, letting Sue command the activities in her kitchen. She was a natural chef.

About an hour later, the food was ready. Sue was delighted with her abilities, and pleased with how well her new side dish turned out. Denise, Donald, Juliana, and Martha carried the food over. Sue fussed about last-minute details; salad dressing, salt and pepper, serving spoons, and napkins. But she had already double-checked those details. She wanted this big meal to be a complete success.

Everyone gathered toward the back of the Exchange and took their seats around the collection of tables. Sue beamed with pride looking at the table of food and the guests for whom she cooked.

Everyone dug in and enjoyed the best meal so far in the new community. They all loved Sue's new side dish and they enjoyed being with each other.

As the sun began to set, the kids and counselors thanked Sue for the food and departed for the cabins. They had movies to watch and found conversation with adults a little boring.

Juliana had conveniently brought Sue's coffee maker to the Exchange. Martha eagerly volunteered to help with the coffee. The others rearranged the chairs back into a circle and sat down to start chatting.

"Those potatoes were really great," Donald complimented Sue. "That was your own recipe? You didn't get it from one of your shows?"

"Nope, it's all mine. I made it myself," Sue proudly told the group.

"It was delicious," Denise added.

"I completely agree," Donald said, looking at Denise.

"Patsy, did you like the food?" Mary asked. "Did you eat this well before?"

"No way. I had burgers and stuff that Dana could get togo from the cafeteria and bring back to me. I never had a sit-down meal like this. This was the best food I've ever eaten."

"Me too," Janet added. "I've never had food like this."

"Larry's wife used to make big meals back when I was on the farm. But they never tasted this good. I agree, this was the best meal."

"Well... I thought it was only *okay*." Carl commented.

"Carl!" Sue stammered, stomping her foot on the floor.

"Just kidding, Sue," Carl replied with his hands up in defense. "You know we all think your cooking is the best."

The smile returned to Sue's face.

"And now, it's time for coffee. Who would like some?" Martha asked.

They all raised their hands, filling Martha with the same good feeling Sue had when cooking and serving the meal. She and Juliana started brewing. They handed out cups as each batch was finished. And they refilled as needed. While they served, the others continued conversing.

"Larry, how'd you like working on a farm?" Carl asked. Did you actually milk the cows?"

"Sure did... I brought them in and hooked 'em up."

Carl laughed at Larry's response.

"What's so funny about milking cows?" Larry wondered.

"It's funny because what you did is the modern way to milk cows," Carl informed him.

"What do you mean?"

"They used to milk cows by hand. They would grab the teats of the cow and squeeze the milk into buckets."

"No! That's not possible," Larry said.

"It is. And that's what they used to do," Carl told him.

"That's not the best way to do it. It probably took a long time for each cow. And it's not clean. What were they thinking?"

"Well, they didn't always have the modern equipment you used. Automated milking has only been used for about thirty or forty years."

"Ah... so that's what the other Larry meant about not having to do it the way his father did," Larry said. "I didn't know what he was talkin' about."

"Patsy, how do you like your coffee?" Mary asked, trying to keep all involved.

"It's pretty good. Better than what we had in the dorm room."

"Did you have coffee a lot?" Mary asked.

"Yeah. Being in college, Dana and her friends, like, hardly ever slept. They stayed awake with coffee while they studied. So I joined them."

"What did Dana study in college?" Sue asked.

"Um... well, I remember some chemistry... atoms and electrons and stuff. And they also had biology... animals and stuff. And history classes, too. I think it was really old history. I didn't really understand any of it. But it was fun to hang with Dana and listen to her and her friends."

Sue dug for more information. "Did her friends think you were different or anything?"

"I didn't talk much so I don't know if they thought I was different. I think Dana said something to them because they didn't ask me many questions about where I came from or why I was there. I think Dana told them I was visiting."

"Where do you think you came from?" Sue asked, digging even deeper.

Carl and Mary were both nervous at Sue's continued curiosity, as they were before, shooting glances at each other and Denise. Denise motioned to them it was okay. They let Sue continue to ask questions.

Patsy, not aware of Carl and Mary's discomfort, responded, "I don't know. I remember Dana was scared and screaming. The guy she was with got her calmed down. They looked at me and looked around the area. Actually... now that I think about it... Dana was also looking at her hand a lot."

"Do you think that was important?"

"I don't know. She wiped her hand on her pants and

then she and the guy tried to figure out what to do about me. It was pretty confusing."

"Did you and Dana talk about what happened?" Sue prodded.

"No. Not really. She kept asking questions when we got to her dorm room but didn't wait for me to answer. But I couldn't have answered. I didn't know the answers to her questions."

Janet added her own history to the discussion, "I heard my person... the other Janet, tell the sheriff about a slime. She said she squeezed a ball that looked like a... tuh... tuhmate--"

"A tomato?" Sue asked.

"Yeah. That's it.... tomato. Janet said she squeezed it and the slime came out on her hand. Then she said I appeared out of nowhere. She kept saying 'out of nowhere'."

"She squeezed a tomato of slime?" Sue asked for clarification.

"That's what she said."

"Hmm..."

Martha unintentionally diverted the conversation by asking, "Anyone want some more coffee?"

"Not if I want to sleep tonight," Patsy responded.

The others agreed with Patsy's assessment.

"Shall we clean up and head back to the houses?" Denise asked everyone.

"I'll help you," Donald volunteered.

"I can help too," Sue offered. "I need dishes for tomorrow's breakfast."

"Might I suggest someone else make breakfast, Sue?" Juliana offered. "Or maybe I can bring some food in to the Exchange tomorrow?"

Sue lowered her eyebrows and shot a look back to her which answered that question without a doubt.

"Okay, okay. I just offered," Juliana replied. "I guess I'll help you clean up your kitchen then. Will you come with me and let Donald and Denise take care of the dishes?"

"Sure," Sue responded with a smile. "Let's go." They left the Exchange and walked across the street.

Everyone did a little bit to clean up. Denise and Donald carried the plates, glasses, and serving dishes back to his house to wash. Patsy, Janet and Larry helped carry the remaining items to Donald's on their way to their own houses. Martha and Juliana took care of the coffee maker and cups. Carl and Mary wiped the tables. The evening ended when everything was clean and back in place.

Chapter 23 - Bookstore Barista

Scrambled eggs, toast, and coffee were ready and waiting on the table for the five adults when they arrived at Sue's house in the morning. As they ate, Sue decided to ask some questions without the ears of the staff listening. "Janet, if it's okay... I'd like to ask you more about the tomato that your look-alike found."

"Okay," Janet agreed.

"Did you hear her describe what happened when you arrived?"

"A little. She said she thought it was a little tomato. She said it was weird because it wasn't green or red. She said it didn't have any color."

"And when she squeezed it, the substance, the slime, came out on her hand? And then you appeared?"

"Yes," Janet replied.

"So... you arrived from substance in a ball. We all arrived from substance on the ground. The substance is the reason we're here. But the ball of substance is new. What does the ball do?"

"Holds the substance," Donald offered.

"Why?" asked Sue.

"For protection," he replied.

"Why didn't each of us have balls of substance?" Sue wondered.

"Maybe we did," suggested Patsy. "Maybe they broke. Dana had the substance on her hand. Maybe she squeezed the ball with her hand and didn't know it."

"So the ball protects the substance," Sue concluded. "But, how did the balls get where they did? If there were balls of substance, how did they get in Sue's garden, or Janet's garden, or the forest at college, or behind the store in Florida, or on a farm in Wisconsin, or in Rockford, or Maryland, or Tennessee, or New York?"

"I don't know," Donald responded. "Does anyone know?"

Silence in the room meant that no one had an idea why the balls of substance were in the locations they were when the residents arrived on the planet.

After sitting and thinking for several minutes, Martha broke the lull by standing up and pouring each a final cup of coffee. The others silently sipped for several minutes, then agreed it was time to get dressed for the day and meet at the Exchange. They each moved slower than usual, because they were thinking about the substance and their arrival.

Within twenty minutes, they emerged from their respective houses and met on Main Street before entering the Exchange together.

When they entered through the doors, a surprise greeted them. Mr. Stevens stood in the front of the store. In his arms was a brand new deluxe coffee maker, still in the box. Martha gave a squeal of delight. She immediately took the box to the back of the Exchange and started setting up. Juliana rushed back to assist her.

Martha read every side of the box before she opened it. She carefully unpacked the contents and, instead of making a batch right away, she took out the operation manual and sat down to read it. She spent ten minutes reading and re-reading to make sure she understood how to use the new appliance.

"This makes twelve cups of coffee and it also makes... es... press--"

"Espresso, it's a thick, dark coffee... really strong," Juliana offered.

"You mean there's more than just regular coffee?"

"Lots more."

"Really? Wow!" She continued reading. "And it can make steam to... froth milk. What's froth?"

"It makes milk bubbly, like a hot whipped cream or... well, it's hard to describe," Juliana told her.

"Then we better make it!" Martha insisted.

They set up the machine and got some ground coffee from the shelves. They made a test batch of brew to learn how the machine worked. They practiced frothing milk and pulled a couple shots of espresso. Then they were ready to start taking orders. Martha walked among the guests who were sitting and talking. A few were adventurous and ordered espresso. The others ordered regular brewed coffee.

Martha and Juliana took their positions at the machine and prepared coffee. Juliana told Martha, "You're a natural barista."

"A what?"

"Barista. It's someone who makes coffee and espresso and stuff at a coffee shop."

"A coffee shop? Like all they make is coffee?"

"Yeah. They serve many different kinds of coffees and cappuccino and espresso and lattes and all that stuff."

"I gotta learn about all that," Martha said excitedly.

"We'll see what we can do," Juliana replied with a smile. She enjoyed watching Martha's excitement. "I'll try to find a book or something you can read."

"Thanks!"

When Martha and Juliana delivered the coffee, the residents and staff sat and sipped. Mr. Stevens came over to say goodbye to all, and Martha repeatedly thanked him for his gift. The others also thanked him, on behalf of Martha. They were glad she had the ability to make coffee whenever and wherever she wanted, not just talk about it.

Blake and TJ took a moment with Mr. Stevens as he headed towards the door to leave. "Sir, the boys are requesting video games," Blake began. "They're getting pretty bored. The number of TV channels is pretty low and they're not very entertaining. And the books aren't popular either."

"Kids can't watch many DVDs without getting restless," TJ added.

"Fine, we can order some games," Ted said flatly.

"The problem is, sir, that game consoles these days are basically computers. You know... like real computers," Blake informed him.

"They connect to the internet," TJ clarified.

"We have wi-fi," Blake said.

Looking confused, Ted asked, "But they can't get access to our network, can they?"

"Not right away," TJ cautiously responded. "But kids are smart. They might figure it out if they have lots of time on their hands."

"Are there any consoles that don't have internet access?"

"Not any modern ones," Blake told Ted.

"I'll think about it, guys," Ted told them. He paused for a moment and then said, "If you can find a way to have the game but keep them from getting internet access, let me know. If the boys are pestering you, tell them I'm working on it. Make no guarantees, but you can tell them I'm at least aware of their request."

"Okay, we'll tell them. Thanks," TJ said.

Mr. Stevens moved to the entrance and waved to all on his way out. The kids and counselors departed for their cabins, snacks and DVDs in hand. Janet, Larry, and Juliana took the opportunity to look for movies for the adults to view in the afternoon. The rest stayed seated, finishing their coffee and talking.

After dinner that evening, the adult residents assembled in the Exchange. Martha went straight to work brewing coffee and making espresso. Janet and Larry walked among the shelves, browsing at the items. The others took seats on the folding chairs in the back.

Mary was on duty, so the others invited her to join them. Mary couldn't refuse a latte from Martha—she was quite good at brewing for only learning how just that morning.

After being served coffee, Sue started the evening's conversation. "Hey Mary, I like the books we have here. But they're for little kids. Can we get some books for older kids? I know that you want to limit what we learn, but we can learn a little more, can't we? Like about the planet and geography?"

"What do you want to know about the planet?" Mary asked.

"Well, you know how all the continents look like they fit together? Did they break apart from one piece of land? It looks like the continents used to fit together, like a puzzle."

"They did," Mary replied. "The crust of the Earth is made up of plates, called tectonic plates. They are different sizes and shapes. The plates shift and slide around the surface of the planet. They really are like big puzzle pieces around the Earth."

"If they're like puzzle pieces, they can't move," Sue argued. "Once you make a puzzle, it's strong because the pieces fit together."

"Ah, but the plates on the Earth don't quite fit together," Mary explained. "There are lots of gaps along the edges. These gaps give the plates room to slide around."

"How do they slide? What makes them move? Aren't the plates really thick?"

"Compared to you and me, yes, they're very thick. But compared to the rest of the planet, they're really thin. They move because of magma. They float and slide around on a layer of magma."

"Magma?" Sue asked.

The others continued to listen silently, very interested in what Mary was saying.

"It's lava, the stuff that comes out of volcanoes. Magma is melted rock."

"So these plates slide on liquid rock?"

"Yes. They slide slowly. But over millions of years, they can move a lot."

Donald joined the discussion. "What happens at the gaps between the plates? Are there big holes on Earth?"

"No holes," Mary replied. "The gaps fill with lava. If you look at the volcanoes around the world, most of them are positioned at the gaps between the plates."

"So the lava comes up through the gaps and that's what volcanoes are?" Donald asked.

"Yes."

"Doesn't the lava cool and get hard and fill in the gaps and seal them up?"

"You would think, Donald. But those gaps are weak. And the plates are still floating on magma. So they're still moving. And the gaps keep cracking."

"If you fill the gaps, doesn't that stop the magma?" Sue asked. When you glue things together, they can't move."

"But lava, the glue, to use your analogy, is weak. It's not super glue. It's not even Elmer's glue. It's like gluing a cardboard puzzle together with cake frosting."

"That wouldn't work," Sue agreed.

"So why does the magma stay melted?" Patsy asked, joining in.

"It keeps coming up from the core of the planet."

"The core of the planet is melted?" Donald asked.

"Yes, Donald. The center of the planet is molten, melted iron. It's liquid metal. And it swirls around. And the heat from the core keeps the outer layer of the planet melted under the crust. So there is always magma under the crust."

Sue summarized what she had heard. "So the plates constantly slide around. And at one time, the continents were one piece, but the plates have cracked and moved and the land has shifted around the planet,"

"Yes," Mary replied with a sigh. "You sure do ask a lot of questions, don't you?"

Sue blushed.

The others thought about the things Mary had told them.

After a few moments of silence in the room, Patsy asked, "But what about the core? How does it stay hot?"

"Yeah, won't it cool?" added Donald. "Food gets cold if you let it sit."

"Well... it will eventually cool down," Mary replied. "After billions of years, it will cool. But for now it's liquid. Gravity keeps it that way. The core is very dense and under lots of pressure from gravity. That pressure keeps the temperature very high. So the core doesn't cool fast."

"What happens when the core cools?" Patsy asked.

"It stops swirling."

"What does that do?"

"The swirling of the iron core maintains the magnetic field around the planet."

"Huh?" Donald asked with a raised eyebrow. He was confused, the same as the others.

"Oh boy," Mary sighed. "This is getting complicated isn't it?"

Sue suggested, "Try to keep it simple."

"Okay." Mary took a deep breath before continuing. "The iron core is magnetic. When it swirls, it creates a magnetic field. That's why the planet has North and South Poles.

"What does the magnetic field do?" Patsy asked.

"It shields the Earth," Mary replied.

"From what?"

"From the dangerous radiation of the sun."

Sue asked, "What would happen if Earth didn't have the magnetic field?"

"The sun's radiation would vaporize the atmosphere. It would disappear. It would basically be zapped into nothing.

All life on Earth would die."

"When will the core cool and the atmosphere go away?" Patsy asked.

"The core will cool in billions of years. But the atmosphere will go away long before that. Humans will take care of that."

"What do you mean?" Donald asked.

"Smog, pollution, carbon dioxide, greenhouse gases, chloro-fluoro-carbons eating away the ozone, stuff like that. Humans are already causing the atmosphere to erode. The temperature on Earth is rising. The planet is dying."

"The planet is *not* dying," Sue firmly interjected with a scowl on her face. "It may be experiencing changes. But Earth is not dying, at least not yet. Trust me."

Everyone looked at Sue with shock. They all wondered why she would make such a bold statement.

Janet and Larry walked over and inadvertently interrupted the silence. They suggested everyone return to Donald's house to watch movies. Everyone considered the proposal and eventually agreed. The residents stood up left together for Donald's house.

Mary silently watched as the group departed. She wondered why Sue reacted so intensely. *What did Sue mean when she said "trust me"? What does Sue know?*

Chapter 24 - Gone

The adults arrived at Sue's house at 7:30 the following morning. They knocked, opened the door and entered as usual.

But there was no smell of coffee. No toast or jam was waiting on the table. No eggs or pancakes were cooking on the stove.

Martha called to Sue. There was no response. She went to Sue's bedroom. Seconds later, Martha returned to the kitchen. "She's gone."

Chapter 25 - Answers

Banging the gavel, the chairman began the meeting. "Can we all take our seats, please? Thank you. Now, we all know why we're here, so let's get started." Turning to Mr. Stevens, he yelled, "Dammit Ted! What the hell happened? We need answers!"

"One of our residents is missing."

"We know that! How? How the hell did it happen?"

"We're not sure. We think she stowed away in a delivery truck to get off the base."

"Where the hell is it now?"

"We don't know. We're trying to find her," Ted calmly answered.

Mr. Wright jumped into the inquisition. "You don't know? Can't you track these aliens? Can't you keep a leash on them?"

"We do not have these people chipped. We can track them no differently than we'd track you or me."

"So you mean that one of these aliens is running around the country, untracked, and has access to... whatever it wants? What the hell can this thing do? How much danger is the public in?"

"These people have learned a lot since being housed

together. I won't deny that. It was inevitable that they share what they know to build the collective knowledge base. But that base of knowledge it still pretty small. The general public is in no danger. I don't think she'll do any harm. But, exactly what she'll do, we're not quite sure."

"This is intolerable!" General Gilmore blustered. "You're housing ticking time bombs; alien bombs that can escape and go off without warning!"

"Please, sir," Ted said, rolling his eyes slightly, annoyed at the general's overreaction. "They have a self awareness and, just like other people, they're trying to explore, to find out what's out there."

"Explorers? That's what these aliens are?" Mr. Mason challenged Ted. "So we're just going to say, 'Oh, okay, go explore. Have fun. Kill our people.' "

"With all due respect, I do not think eleven people, five of them children, can take over the world. That is not their motive."

"Oh, really? Then please tell us, Ted, what is their motive?" the chairman asked.

Ted squirmed a bit in his chair. He didn't know. But he tried to calm the tension by assuring the committee that "their motive" was not dangerous. "We can't be certain right now. From everything we've seen so far, they are not unstable and have shown no tendency for violence. They are likely either just curious, or maybe they have larger goal, something simple, like a message to deliver."

"A message? Like 'Hello, we're here to kill you.' Or 'Live long and prosper until the fleet arrives.' You mean something simple like that?" the general snapped. "Ted, you have brought nothing to this committee except promises to contain and limit knowledge. But one of the goddamn things knew enough to get out and is now loose! What the hell are we supposed to do?"

Ted rubbed his temples in frustration. "The first thing we're going to do is find the one that escaped. We've already increased security at the base."

Sarcastically, the general prodded, "Oh well, thank goodness you increased security. We wouldn't want *another* one to escape! Two would be so much worse than one alien on the loose."

"Sir, please," Ted responded with a shake of his head. "We'll find her and interview her to find out why she left the base."

"Just talk? That's it? That's all? We're going to tell them 'Please don't do it again.' Is that all we're going to do? Dammit, Ted! We need real action!"

Sighing, Ted dejectedly caved to the committee. "We can chip them and separate them. We can restrict access to all information. In short, the base will be a prison."

"Okay! Now *that's* action!" the general roared.

"But they have done no crime," Ted protested in one last try for a balanced response.

"The aliens invaded our planet, didn't they? Now get out there and find that goddamn alien!"

Ted dropped his shoulders. "We'll find it, sir."

Chapter 26 - Mission

Outside the truck stop, Sue talked to many drivers. She was trying to find a ride east, closer to her destination, but she had no money. She hoped someone would be nice enough to give her a ride.

She obviously hadn't slept, and she didn't look or act like she belonged there. Some drivers ogled her. Others ignored her. Some warned her that it was not safe to solicit rides at a truck stop.

A tall, skinny, old man driving a Frito-Lay truck listened to Sue's request for a ride. Recognizing Sue was penniless and in need of some help, he agreed to take Sue to Oklahoma City. He escorted Sue to his truck and helped her climb in. Sue was nervous, being confined in a vehicle with a stranger, but she had a mission to complete. She'd take the chance.

"You look tired ma'am," the driver observed. "It's a long drive to Oklahoma City. Try to get some sleep. We might stop in Albuquerque. I'll wake you up if we do."

"Thank you, sir," Sue replied. "I appreciate you helping me."

As the semi truck pulled out of the truck stop, Sue leaned against the door and gazed out the window, recalling how she got where she was.

When the other residents had left her house after watching the movie, she took a walk and noticed a plain white delivery truck dropping off supplies on the side of the Exchange. The driver had left the rear door open.

She turned out the lights in her house, walked out the door, and walked across Main Street. On the side of the Exchange in the shadow of the street light, she climbed in the empty delivery truck and moved to the back. She hoped the driver wouldn't see her.

When the driver finished his delivery, he came around the back of the truck, tossed in empty boxes, reached up, to grab the handle, and closed the door. He didn't even look in the back.

The engine started and the truck began to move. After a short drive and a few turns to get to the freeway, it reached its cruising speed. She tried to sleep while listening to the constant sound of the engine in the dark, but she couldn't. She was too nervous and scared.

When the truck stopped, she waited for a minute before moving to the rear door. She held her breath, and slowly pulled up on the door. It opened. *Thank goodness!* She climbed out of the empty truck, closed the door, and quickly walked to the side of the nearest building. She had no idea where she was.

She observed men walking in and out of the building, to and from trucks. After several minutes, she got up the courage to investigate. The tourist pamphlets in the display case just inside the front doors of the building told her she was in Flagstaff, Arizona. *But how far is this from where I started? How much farther until I complete my mission?*

When she saw the delivery truck drive away, she knew there was no going back to her house at the base. She had to keep going.

Sue didn't wake up until the Frito-Lay truck stopped. "We're in Albuquerque," the driver informed her. "Stay here ma'am. I'll get us both something to eat and bring it back here to the truck."

"I don't have any money to pay for my food."

"Most people who hitchhike don't. Don't worry about it." The driver closed the door and walked to the truck stop diner in the noon-day sun.

Sue waited in the cab of the truck for the driver to come back. She didn't touch anything, or even look around much. She just thought about what she had to do.

The driver returned in twenty minutes with two cheeseburgers and fries. "I hope these will be okay. Not very healthy, but they sure taste good. I didn't know what you wanted on your burger--"

"Mustard."

"So I brought packets of ketchup and mustard and mayonnaise for you," the driver continued.

"Oh. Thank you," she said. A little shame showed on her face. After surveying the food, Sue commented, "This looks good. They fried the potatoes. They're crispy. And this cheeseburger is really large. They put lettuce on it. This looks really good."

Sue devoured her meal and finished her soda. She sat back in the passenger seat and decided that truck stop food was good food. She mentally made a note to remember to stop at truck stops whenever possible... if she ever got the chance in the future.

"My name is Pat," the driver said. "May I ask your name?"

"Sue."

"You seem to have left in a hurry, Sue. No bags, or change of clothes, or anything."

"Yes, I left last night. But I can't say where."

131

"It's okay. I'm not trying to pry. I'm just making small talk. What do you plan to do in Kansas?"

"Go visit my old family."

"A little reunion, eh? What do you have planned?"

"I don't know what will happen. But I know I need to see them."

"Urgent message from home, eh?"

"Message..."

She faded into thought, not remembering she was in the middle of a conversation with Pat.

Seeing her attention fade off into the distance, Pat said, "I guess we'll get going on to Oklahoma."

Sue heard the driver and told him, "I'm sorry, Pat. I didn't mean to be rude. I just have a lot of thoughts in my head."

"I don't think you're rude," he said with a smile. "You obviously got a lot on your mind. Care to listen to some music?"

Sue nodded in agreement and Pat turned on a disc of country music. She seemed to like the selection because she tapped her feet in rhythm until she fell asleep.

Sue woke, as before, when the truck stopped. She looked around to get her bearings. It was early morning. She had slept all night. She hadn't even realized that Pat had stopped along the way to get a few hours of sleep.

"Here we are in Oklahoma City," Pat told her.

"We're here already?"

"You slept through the whole trip from Albuquerque."

"I'm sorry," she apologized. I wasn't much of a guest. I was bad company."

"No need to apologize. I'm glad I could help by getting you this far without you having to worry about it. C'mon. I'll take you inside and we'll see if we can find you a ride up to Kansas."

Sue accompanied Pat into the truck stop restaurant. Pat waved to a few fellow drivers he knew and walked over to talk with them. Sue took a seat on a stool at the counter.

"What'll ya have, hun?" the waitress asked.

"What? Huh?" Sue mumbled, startled by the waitress' question.

"You here to eat, or just take a load off?"

"I don't have any money with me."

"You can't go far on that, sweetie."

Pat approached Sue and the waitress, along with another driver. "Hi ya, Marge! What's new?"

"Not much, just the same ol', same ol'. I'm overworked, underpaid, and short of help. Oh well, I get by just seeing all your faces each week."

"Sue, this is Mr. K.," Pat introduced. "I told him he'd be doing you and me a favor by driving you to Kansas. He has kindly agreed."

Mr. K. was average height and above average weight. He wore jeans, a t-shirt, and a full black beard peppered with grey whiskers. He had a smile on his face when he approached Sue.

"Thank you Mr. K. I appreciate it, a lot," Sue told him.

"No sweat, Sue. I owe Pat a favor or two."

"So, should we have a bite?" Pat asked.

"I'd like that," Sue replied. But as I told Marge, I don't have any money on me."

"No problem," Pat responded. I'll spring for another burger."

"No. I can't let you do that," Sue protested. "I can wait until I get to Kansas." She turned on the stool and looked down at the floor. Quietly she added, "I wish I could cook my dinner."

"What's that you said, hun?" Marge asked. "Cook your own dinner? You know how to cook?"

She looked up at Marge and replied, "Some things. Yes. I can cook."

"I tell you what," Marge proposed, "you help me in the

kitchen for, let's say, four hours, to get through the breakfast rush, and I'll let you make your own lunch, free of charge. How's that sound, Sue? Can you spare the time, K.?"

"That sounds like a great idea. I'd love to!" Sue eagerly agreed.

Seeing Sue's excitement, Mr K. replied, "Yeah... I got time. Go ahead."

"Well, come on back here, Sue," Marge called out. "Let's get cooking!"

Sue walked behind the counter and joined Marge in the kitchen. She washed her hands, put on an apron and a hair net. Marge introduced Sue to the other short-order cook, Joe, and told him Sue would lend a hand for a few hours. Marge winked at him and he understood.

"Now, Sue, what can you cook?"

After her four-hour shift was over, Sue emerged from the kitchen and walked into the dining area with a smile on her face.

From behind the lunch counter, Marge complimented Sue. "You did a great job, hun. Thanks a ton for filling in."

A customer seated at the counter added his compliments to Marge's, "Sue, this spaghetti is delicious. Thanks for suggesting it."

"It's got extra garlic, oregano and thyme in the sauce." Sue noted.

"It tastes like authentic Italian," the customer exclaimed.

Another customer also gave his critique, "Sue, the omelet tastes great! Marge, how long is Sue staying? You should hire her."

Everyone in the restaurant was energized by Sue's cooking and Sue smiled from ear to ear after hearing the compliments. This was the happiest she had ever been in her short life.

Marge responded to the customer's suggestion, "Sorry,

Phil, she's gotta go out of town." Turning to Sue, she said, "Now, go make yourself something for the road, sweetie, and Mr. K. will get you on your way."

Sue made her meal; two cheeseburgers, topped with spicy mustard and sliced pickles, a large order of fries and an extra-large coke. On her way out of the restaurant, she repeatedly thanked Marge.

She and Mr. K. left the truck stop and he led her to his truck. Sue climbed into the passenger seat of his truck with her food. She showed Mr. K. the two cheeseburgers and told him one was for him. She thanked him again for waiting until she finished working and for taking her to Enterprise.

"Enterprise?" Mr. K. asked, surprised. "I'm driving to Kansas City."

"Are they not close?"

"Not exactly. To get to Enterprise, I'll have to go up I-one-thirty-five to interstate seventy instead of up I-thirty-five and three-thirty-five to Topeka. It'll add some time to my route."

"Oh please Mr. K., if you can get me to Enterprise without having to take another truck, I'd be... well, I can't really explain how happy I'd be. I'd be very happy. I have to get to my old family... to a reunion. And I need to get there quickly."

He sighed and shook his head. "Okay, I can drop you off a couple miles from Enterprise, where I-seventy meets Highway forty three. You can walk from there."

"Oh, thank you Mr. K."

"Let's get rolling."

Chapter 27 - Ted

Ted was stunned. He was a Zombie.

He got into the black sedan, rode to the air field, boarded the plane, sat down, and buckled his belt without making eye contact with anyone. He was lost in his mind.

What have I got myself into?

'Dammit Ted, we can't have these aliens running around killing people!'

Don't you think I know that? What do they think I am, an idiot?

But they're not running around and they're not going to kill anyone... I don't think.

No. They are *not* going to kill anyone. I know it. That's not their end game. They won't harm anyone. They're not going to take over the planet. I know it. I've seen them. I can feel it.

But now I have to chip them and separate them, because I told the committee I would.

Why did I do that? I got my ass kicked, that's why I did it. I have to do it because we don't know enough about them or what they want. So we have to lock 'em up like criminals.

'They invaded our planet! That's their crime!'

So are they enemy combatants? Is our base the new alien prison? Will we keep them there until they die? No trial? No release?

And they're happy about it. They even want to name their prison! They want to name it Independent, U.S.A. because they think they're independent. How far away from the truth can that be? They're not independent. They're prisoners!

And we cut them off from all sources of knowledge. We rot their brains away.

And now we have to track them... wherever they go.

Wherever they go? What, walking around their house and going to the bathroom? What good would a chip do? It's so we can track them when they escape.

When... Why not if? *If* we can keep them from leaving, we don't need to chip them. We just lock them down in their prison.

This is insane! They aren't going to take over the world! But yet... we do have to find out what they are going to do.

Do... when? When they get out? But they're not going to get out.

But we have an escapee. They *can* get out.

'Hunt it down! Find it! Don't let it kill anyone!'

It...

She's not an 'it'. Sue is not an 'it'!

Oh my God! I called her 'it' in the meeting! What have I become? In one short meeting, those bastards had me thinking like them!

Screw 'em. I'm not going to do it. I'm not going to lock those people up. They're human beings! Yes, they *are*! They may have different origins, but they're people!

So what do I have to do? I *do* have to get Sue back... safely. And I've got to stay at the base. I've got to insert myself into their community. I have to figure out what they want. Figure out why they're here. Figure out what we can do for them.

Oh boy, I'm screwed. I'm not going to do what I was ordered. And I might even enable Sue and the others. What if I end up helping them take over the world?

Ted, you *are* an idiot if you think they're here to take over the world. There are eleven residents. Eleven versus three hundred million in the US, or eleven versus six billion in the world... either way... fair fight, right?

No. I'm sure they have a different purpose. I'm going to figure it out. I am *going* to figure it out.

Now, how do I find Sue? Where did she go? She only knows of one other place... Kansas.

Suddenly snapping out of his zombie haze, he pushed his com button and gave instructions to the flight crew. "We need to go to Kansas. Get me as close to Enterprise as you can."

"That's not our itinerary, Ted. I'm not authorized to do that," the pilot responded. "We're scheduled to land in California."

"I'm a Division Head in an office of Homeland Security. I report to the Undersecretary of the department. That should be enough clearance to change the itinerary."

"Um... I don't think so, sir," replied the pilot.

"Well then... who might be authorized?"

"I've never changed my itinerary in mid-flight, sir."

"Then I think it's now time you did. We have intelligence that the security breach which originated in California is now in Kansas, heading for Enterprise. Get me as close to there as possible... land at a civilian airport if you have to. We're registered as private, so no one should notice. You are hereby authorized. I take full responsibility. If you want to fly to California after you drop me off, you are free to do that."

"He should have the authority," the co-pilot told the pilot. "He is the director of a Division."

"You're probably right... I think. Okay, we'll make the change with air traffic control. We should land in about an hour," the pilot responded. "But I'm not taking the fall for this, Ted. It's your ass on the line."

"Thank you, gentlemen," Ted replied. "Now, I need to make some calls."

Chapter 28 - Convergence

Sue and Mr. K. passed the trip with pleasant conversation. She didn't want him to ask personal questions and he didn't want information. They talked about tornadoes, the dust bowl, the Rocky Mountains and other geological and meteorological topics. When they reached the junction of I-70 and Hwy 43, Mr. K. pulled over.

"This is where I drop you off. If you follow this road, Highway forty three, for about two miles, you'll reach Enterprise."

"Thank you Mr. K. I really *really* appreciate it. You have been a huge help."

"I hope all is well with you and your family."

"So do I," she said with a nervous look. Changing to a smile, she told her driver, "Thank you. I won't forget you, even if I never see you again. And tell Pat, when you see him, and Marge too, that I won't forget them either. Goodbye Mr. K."

She climbed out of the truck and started walking south with determination. She was only a few miles from her destination. She was almost done with her mission.

After a few minutes of walking in the late afternoon sun, she was approached by a car driving toward her. It passed her on the highway, and then its tires squealed as the driver slammed on the brakes. The car was a sheriff's cruiser driven by Spike. He got out of the car and walked toward Sue, who was several hundred feet away. He yelled at her, "What are you doing walking on the highway? Where's your car? What happened? Who's with Karen?"

"Hi Spike. It's me, the other Sue," she called out.

He stopped in the middle of the road, shocked. "What the hell are you doing back here?"

"I have to talk to Susan and Karen... and to David and Petunia and you. I have a message."

"From who? About what?"

"Take me to Susan's house and I'll tell you."

They walked toward each other on the highway. "What if I call Ted Stevens instead?" Spike asked.

"Please do. I'm sure he's already on his way here. He must know I'm not at my house. So while we wait for him to arrive, why don't you take me to Susan's house?"

Spike paused to consider her proposal. Realizing Sue was correct about Ted, and knowing they couldn't carry on a conversation standing in the middle of Highway forty-three, he told her to follow him to his car. They walked to the cruiser and got in.

On the way to Susan's house, Sue explained how she left the base and hitched rides. She also told Spike about her shift at the truck stop. It had been a while since he saw this Sue, so he had trouble truly understanding how much this new person had absorbed and learned. She left Enterprise as a six year-old, and returned as an adult.

As they passed the driveway of David Hudson, Spike stopped the car and honked. David came around the corner of the house. Spike yelled out the window, "Meet me at Susan Robert's house right away! And call Petunia and have her meet at Susan's as well! Hurry!"

Around the corner, they pulled into Susan's driveway. Spike honked the horn. Karen and Susan came out of the house and walked toward the car. Spike got out of the car and said hello. And then Sue got out.

Karen's eyes lit up. A friend had returned.

Susan went ashen. A nightmare had returned.

The four were soon joined by Petunia and David. Upon their arrival, Sue asked if they could all go inside where she'd explain her mission. No one disagreed. They entered the house and all sat in the front room, except Sue, who remained standing.

"You're the people who know of my existence. That's why I've come back," Sue began.

As she talked, a red compact car quickly rounded the corner and pulled into the driveway. (A black sedan was not available on short notice.) A man in a black suit crawled out of the car. He didn't bother with his black portfolio.

He walked up to the house and looked into the front window. He could see Spike and the others sitting on the couch and chairs facing Sue. Sue's back was toward the window. He couldn't see her face. She couldn't see him.

He voiced his thoughts about what to do. "What is she doing? Spike has his gun. He hasn't drawn it. He and David look calm. I can ring the bell or go around the back and sneak in. What should I do? Ring the doorbell. It will provide a distraction if Spike needs it." Ted rang the doorbell.

Sue answered the door. "Hello Mr. Stevens," she said pleasantly. "You finally arrived. I expected you would. Come in."

Ted entered in silence. He made eye contact with Spike and David to detect any indication of trouble. Their eyes gave no sign of concern.

"Good evening, Ted," Susan said. "Sue, here, was just telling us why she came back."

If ever a person's jaw could actually drop to the floor, this was one of those instances. Ted couldn't speak. He had no idea what to say. He just stood in the front room, stunned.

"Please take a seat. I see you need it," Susan continued. "Let us fill you in."

Spike reassured him, "Everything is fine."

"I was telling my family," Sue told Ted, motioning to the people in the room, "that I had to come back to tell them about my existence. I needed to come back since they are the ones who know of me and how I arrived."

She looked at each person and said, "When you first met me, I was young and didn't know anything about Earth. But I was always aware of something. Like a thought that kept repeating in my head. But I had no idea what it was.

"When I stayed here at the house, I started reading everything I could. I learned as much as I could about Earth, as much as Karen's books would tell me.

"When you moved me to my house, Ted, I learned a lot more from the others. I learned about how they arrived on the planet. I figured out the substance was where we all came from.

"But it wasn't until we had the discussion with Mary at the Exchange that the message became clear. She said the planet was dying. And I told her it wasn't. She looked at me like I was... I don't know... weird. But I knew. I know Earth is not dying. Not like the other planet."

Ted and the others looked at Sue as if she had grown a second head. They were shocked to hear her talk of another planet, a dying planet.

"The substance was sent from a planet a long way away," Sue continued. "I don't know where. I don't know the name of the planet or what people lived there. But I know that they died. The planet died. To save the people, they sent the substance. The memory of those people is in the substance. I don't know if Earth people... us... the residents at the base, can extract the knowledge completely, but at least the people from the planet did not die without someone else knowing."

"So the lab was right," Ted said out loud to himself. "There was a message in the substance, hidden in the DNA." Turning to Sue, he asked, "How do you know that it's only a message? Is it something else? How do you know that it won't become a mutation? How do you know that the message won't become a new behavior that you and the others will exhibit? How do you know you won't go crazy and attack people?"

"I don't."

Silence filled the room.

Looking at the others in the room, Sue smiled and finished, "Thank you for letting me deliver my message. I hope this is not the last time I see you. Now, Mr. Stevens, please escort me home."

Not knowing what else could be discussed, Ted shrugged his shoulders and silently nodded, agreeing to escort Sue back to the base. He reached a hand out and guided Sue to the door. On his way, he told Spike he'd keep him updated.

As Ted opened the door to leave, Karen spoke for the first time that evening. "What are you going to do to Sue?"

"I'm going to take Sue back to her house."

"What's going to happen to her? You better not hurt my friend. She's my sister!"

An awkward look came over Ted's face. He had no intention of harming Sue, but yet, he had no idea what Sue and the others might do. He asked himself, "What if I'm forced to take action? I can't lie to the girl."

He looked into Karen's eyes and saw her determination. He pondered the consequences. *I would never be able to return to Enterprise if I don't reassure her now. And I'd never be able to return if Sue was hurt by anybody.* He knew the correct answer.

He smiled and replied to Karen, "I won't hurt Sue. I promise."

Chapter 29 - Options

Sue and Ted boarded the jet and took seats at the table near the back. The co-pilot closed the door and moved to the cockpit. Ted told the pilots to fly back to the base. He sat in silence and tried to understand what had happened. He hadn't yet talked to Sue.

Sue also sat in silence, unsure of how Ted would react.

The plane taxied to the runway and took off.

Ted sighed, rubbed his head, and finally spoke, "So Sue, please help me understand what happened."

"Okay."

"How did you leave the base?"

"I climbed into a delivery truck that left the Exchange. I got out when it stopped at a truck stop."

"Where was that? Do you know?"

"Yes. Flagstaff Arizona."

"And then...?"

"I found someone to drive me to Kansas. Pat drove me to Oklahoma City. Then Mr. K. drove me to Enterprise."

"I see. How did you eat?"

"I didn't until Albuquerque. Pat bought me food. Then I worked at the truck stop in Oklahoma City. Marge let me work for my dinner."

"What? You worked for your food?" Ted shook his head in disbelief. "Where?"

"In Marge's restaurant," she replied with a proud smile. "I made spaghetti and burgers and sandwiches and eggs and pancakes and fries. Everyone liked my cooking."

"And in exchange... er... Marge is it? ...gave you a free meal?"

"I had no money."

"And what else happened?" Ted asked, expecting more.

"That's about it. I got to see Oklahoma and Kansas."

Ted paused, digesting all he had heard Sue, and then said, "Tell me again about your message. You knew you had a message, but you didn't know what it was, correct?"

"Yes."

"But as you talked with Donald, Martha and the boys, you realized the substance was the reason you appeared?"

"Yes, and Patsy, Janet, and Larry. I heard you all talking about a substance so I knew it was related to all of us."

"So you were listening, weren't you? We didn't think you could understand."

"Please, Mr. Stevens," she said lowering her eyebrows and glaring at Ted, "Never think we can't understand."

"I won't from now on," Ted told her while holding up his hands. He continued, "And the message in the substance informed you that you're from a species that died when their planet died."

"Yes."

"How do you know this? How can substance turn into people who have messages from an alien species that's dead?"

"I don't know how. But I know it's true," she replied confidently.

"What else is the message telling you?"

"Nothing that I know of. But maybe it'll tell us something in the future," Sue suggested.

Ted slapped his hands on the table. "You see! That's what I'm worried about!" Ted exclaimed.

"Why?"

"What are you all going to do in the future?" Flailing his hands, he anxiously asked, "What if you go crazy and try to take over the world?"

"We're six adults and five kids," Sue flatly responded.

"What if there are more we haven't found, more of you around the world?"

"There might be more of us, but not enough to take over the world."

"What about procreation?"

"Huh?" Sue asked, confused.

"What if you have kids?"

"Me?"

"All of you."

"How do we have kids? You mean Kati and Violet?"

"Er..."

"Oh!" Sue realized what Ted meant. "Do you mean new kids? Like babies?"

"Yes."

"How does that happen?" Sue asked.

"Uh... let's not get into that right now," Ted said. "Let's assume that you all have kids. What might happen then?"

"More people," Sue calmly answered.

"That's what scares us," Ted said, trying to reason with Sue.

"Why?"

"More alien messages in the world."

"Yes. But there's still only a few of us. What can we do?"

"That's the problem," Ted said, mainly to himself. "There are too many unknowns."

"So what are you going to do?" Sue asked.

Ted sat and thought for a while. Sue sat patiently and waited for him to speak. Finally, he said, "Well, there are a couple options."

"What are they?"

"I'm afraid I can't go into details," Ted told her, shaking

his head.

"It's simple," Sue concluded. "You can either keep us at the base forever or let us live where we want."

Ted sighed and dropped his shoulders, but did not respond. Sue was correct.

"We just want to live like normal people," she told him. "But you're afraid that we'll do something in the future, like go and attack everyone on Earth... which you know is not possible. But you have to keep the U.S. safe and keep us at the base forever. Yes, I can see your options."

Again, Ted sat, slumped in his seat, silently thinking. He heard what Sue had said.

The hum of the jet engines was the only sound in the cabin for several minutes. Finally, Ted sat up straight, raised his head, and looked resolutely at Sue. "No," he said. "There's only one option. Excuse me, Sue. I need to make a couple phone calls." He moved to the bench seat in the front of the plane and picked up the satellite phone receiver to make some calls.

About an hour later, the plane landed at the base. Ted and Sue deplaned in silence and were driven by the co-pilot to Sue's house. All was quite at the base, everyone was asleep. Sue got out of the car, said goodnight to Ted, and entered her house. Ted stood by the car and stared into the night. He knew what he had to do.

Chapter 30 - Because of Sue

At 7:30 the next morning, there was a knock at Sue's front door. But it wasn't the other residents arriving for breakfast. It was Ted. She opened the door. "Good morning Sue."

"Hello Mr. Stevens."

"Might I ask you to join all of us in the Exchange?"

"Can I have five minutes to get dressed?"

"Yes, please. See you in a few minutes." Ted turned and walked across the lawn, crossed Main Street, and entered the Exchange.

Sue got dressed and walked across the street. She entered the building and walked to the back. Everyone, residents and staff, sat in a big circle of chairs. She took the last seat.

Scanning the faces of all seated in the circle of chairs, Ted began the meeting. "First of all, as you can see, Sue has returned from her little vacation. We can all hear her stories after this meeting, so please hold your questions. Second, thank you all for assembling this early in the morning. Martha, you can make us all coffee in a little bit. Now, why we're all here..." Thinking of how best to say what he came to say, Ted paused, scratched the back of his head, and then took a deep breath. He sighed and told everyone, "We're here because of Sue."

The residents and staff looked to Sue to see if she gave any clue what Ted meant. She simply shrugged her shoulders.

"You see…" Ted continued, "Sue forced me to make a decision much earlier than I had hoped. She knows about where you all came from and why you all are here. She left the base and went back to the place of her origin. She told her old family and friends in Kansas about all of you and how you all arrived. And then she gave those people your message, the message of the extinct species from the dead planet."

The staff members all looked at Ted, confused. The residents all looked to each other and hesitantly smiled.

"Now all of that is out in the general public. People know that you carry an alien message. So what am I supposed to do?" He paused, looking at each of the residents.

The residents waited for Ted to continue.

"As Sue deduced," Ted told them, "there are two options. One is to let you all free to live however you want and spread your message at will. The other is to keep you here at the base forever so you cannot further interact with Earth's population."

Ted waited to see if there was any reaction from the residents or the staff. There was nothing but silence. They all sat, looking at him with anticipation of his next comment. He stood up straight. "I've decided you're all free to leave."

A collective gasp echoed throughout the Exchange. The staff didn't know how to react. The residents looked to each other with smiles, but also uncertainty.

"You're letting us go?" Sue asked, wide-eyed in disbelief.

"Wherever we want?" asked Donald excitedly.

"We can do what we want?" Martha confirmed happily.

The residents all smiled at each other, hoping that what Ted had told them was true.

"Yes," Ted said to all, smiling at the resident's reactions.

He raised his hands to ask all for quiet and calm. "But there are a few things before you all leave. I need you all to listen very carefully. Today we'll be receiving a couple deliveries. The first is twenty comfortable chairs to put here in our little bookstore café. The second delivery is eleven laptop computers and two Xbox video game consoles."

"What?" Carl exclaimed. "You're giving them computers?"

"Yes," Ted replied calmly, looking at Carl. He turned to the residents and said, "And we're going to give them unrestricted access to the internet."

"What?" TJ asked. "Why?"

"As a colleague of mine once said, 'You can find anything on the internet.'"

"Uh... Ted... I don't..." Mary stuttered.

Raising his hand, Ted explained his decision to the staff. "Here's the deal. We can't keep everyone contained here at the base. We cannot keep eleven people locked up forever." Looking to the residents, he continued. "You are not dangerous. You're self-aware. You know where you came from. We cannot lock you up forever." He paused to look at everyone's reaction. "But," he added, "we can't let you go out into the world without preparation. You can prepare by learning as much as you can. And the best way is to surf the internet and learn with, and from each other." The room remained silent. "Now, Martha... how about some coffee?"

Martha jumped up and rushed over to start making coffee. Juliana got up to assist.

"Before you help her, Juliana," Ted interjected, "can I have a word with you and the rest of the staff? Please join me over by the front doors."

The staff stood and walked with Ted to the front of the Exchange. After checking to see that no resident was within earshot, Ted bent down like a quarterback in a huddle. The others followed his lead.

"None of this gets out," he firmly told his staff members, looking into each person's eyes. "No one is to let anyone outside of us know what the plan is. If word gets out to the Department, none of you will ever get another job again. Understand? My butt is so far over the line, I'm sure this is the last job I'll ever have. But you know this is the correct decision. This is the correct thing to do. Do you all agree?"

Each of the staff took a few moments to consider Ted's question, and then confidently nodded in agreement.

"I'll communicate with DHS. But I won't let them know until I have to. I'll cover for you all, I promise. It's my decision and I'll personally take the fall for it. The most important thing is to take care of our guests. Now, let's go have breakfast."

The staff slowly broke their huddle. They were confused about what had just happened, but each knew Ted's decision was correct; letting the residents go was the only option. They had spent enough time with the residents to know they weren't going to harm anyone. They all knew they couldn't keep these people locked up.

Denise walked back to the chairs and called to Sue. Sue broke off her conversation with the other residents. "We've got a lot of cooking to do," Denise told her.

Sue smiled from ear to ear as she picked up supplies from the shelves and refrigerators.

Watching Sue and Denise exit the Exchange to make breakfast at Sue's house, Donald followed to assist.

After eating, Ted found a quiet corner of the Exchange to work. The staff noticed he didn't leave the base.

The residents pushed the folding chairs to the open area for the last time. They sat down on the hard, noticeably uncomfortable chairs. They could hardly wait the few hours until the new chairs would be delivered.

Martha made another pot of coffee and took espresso orders. As she worked, she called out, "Sue, are you going to tell us what happened?"

"Yeah, what did you do, Sue?" asked Janet. "How did you get out?"

"I sneaked out in a truck that was delivering something here at night. And then other truck drivers took me to my family's home in Kansas."

"You got into one of the delivery trucks?" Mary asked, shocked.

"Yes. I saw it by the Exchange in the light from the lamp on Main Street."

"And you left your house and just climbed in the truck?" Mary continued. "What made you do that?"

"I don't know exactly," Sue replied honestly. "But I had to deliver my message. I knew the truck would leave the base. And I knew that I needed to leave the base to go see my old family. So I guess I knew I had to get into the truck. I hoped it would stop where I could get out and find a way to Kansas."

"Weren't you afraid of being discovered in the truck?" Donald asked.

"Not really. Not at first. After I rode for a while and thought about what I had done, I started to get worried, but I had to get to Kansas so it didn't really matter."

"Where did the truck stop?" Denise continued.

"At a truck stop, of course. I waited until the driver got out, then I snuck out of the back of the truck. I looked around the building and talked to people coming out to ask them for a ride."

"You just asked truck drivers to take you to your family?" Larry asked.

"I asked lots of drivers to take me as far towards Kansas as they could. Most drivers wouldn't even talk to me. But I found a really nice man, Pat. He bought me dinner and took me to Oklahoma City. Then Mr. K. took me from Oklahoma City to Enterprise Kansas, where my family lives."

"And did I hear Ted say that you worked in a restaurant?" Patsy confirmed. "Like, a real restaurant?"

"Yep. I had no money to buy food. But Marge let me work there. It was great! Lots of customers said I made good food," she told the others, smiling with pride.

"When you visited your family, what did you tell them?" Donald asked.

"I told them what we all know. We appeared from a substance sent from a planet that died a long time ago. We have messages in us that tell the story of the people on the planet. Or at least that tell us the people once existed."

The residents thought about the message. After hearing Ted say they all had a message to deliver, and hearing Sue say it just then, they each silently nodded as if they knew it all along. They realized what Sue figured out a few days ago; they are the remaining voices for an extinct species.

"What did your family say when you told them?" Donald continued.

"Nothing. I'm not sure they believed me," Sue said plainly. "If they did, they probably didn't know what to say to me."

"And what did Mr. Stevens say?" Donald asked.

"He believed me… I think. I told him everything I know."

"Is he in trouble because you escaped?" Patsy wondered.

"I don't know… maybe. He'll probably be in trouble when he lets us go," Sue suggested.

"Why?" Janet asked.

"Because they moved us here to keep us here, so we couldn't attack everyone and take over the world."

"But we wouldn't do that." Larry said, irritated at the notion.

"We all know that, Larry. But Mr. Stevens and his superiors don't know that. That's why we're here. But now he knows we won't attack anyone, so he's letting us go."

"What will happen to him?" Janet asked.

She shrugged her shoulders and replied, "I don't know."

After some thought, Donald insisted, "We have to help him. We have to help Mr. Stevens."

"I agree," Sue said immediately. "Do we all agree?" she asked the others. All the residents nodded in agreement. "So how do we help him?"

They all tried to come up with ideas about what they might do, but no ideas quickly came to mind.

"What do his superiors think will happen if we're let go?" Donald asked.

"Attack people," replied Sue.

"Why would we do that?"

"We wouldn't. But they think we would. So they want us locked up."

"How do we show them we don't mean any harm?" Patsy wondered.

"I don't know," Sue responded.

Their conversation was disrupted by the arrival of the new sitting chairs. Everyone hastily pushed the folding chairs aside as the delivery men emptied the truck and brought the chairs in. As the chairs were put in place, the residents and staff all sat down. They relaxed for a few minutes and relished the comfort. Martha thought this was an excellent opportunity for more coffee.

With the temporary disruption over, Donald resumed the conversation. "Where were we?"

Patsy replied, "Um... I think we were trying to convince Mr. Stevens we won't take over the world."

"How do we know we're not actually here to take over the world?" Brandy wondered. Everyone looked at her with surprise. "Duh! I'm not suggesting we do it," Brandy said, offended. "But, you know, the message Sue got took time to get to her... or for her to be aware of it. How do we know there won't be more messages?"

"We don't," Donald concluded.

Sue told the others, "In Kansas, Mr. Stevens said, 'The lab was right. There was a message in the substance, hidden in the DNA.' What's DNA?"

Mary joined the discussion. "It's the genetic messages inside each cell of your body that tells the cell what to do.

DNA is the code that makes each of us who we are."

"Is DNA the same for everybody?" Sue asked.

"Every person has slightly different genetic material from every other person. Your DNA makes you unique."

"So we got our DNA from the substance?"

"Your DNA probably came from your other people, the people that touched the substance. That's why you look like them." Pointing to all the residents, she said, "You are exact copies of them. You're clones."

"So we have DNA from our people. But we also have a message from the substance too… a message about the other species and their planet."

"That might be true. But the message might not be in your DNA," Mary said.

"So how do we prove that our DNA doesn't also have a message to take over the world?"

Mary stopped to think. While she did, the others sat patiently in silence, waiting for her to come up with a solution. After several moments, she resumed eye contact with the residents and offered a suggestion. "The substance had a message in the DNA about the species and their planet. And the message was transferred to you. But maybe the DNA wasn't transferred. Maybe the message came to you when you transformed from your other people. Maybe you only have your other people's DNA and no extra. The only way to know is to go look for extra DNA in you."

"I'm not sure I understand," Donald said. "How would we know we don't have any messages?"

"We don't," Mary replied. "But if you have the *same* DNA as your other person, and no *extra* DNA, there is no obvious sign of a message."

"So same is good?" Sue asked.

"This is tricky," Mary admitted. "If your DNA matches your other person's DNA exactly, no more, no less, you're identical. And no one thinks your other people have messages to take over the world."

"What if we do have extra DNA?" Donald asked.

"If your genetic material contains extra DNA, we can't say you don't have any other messages, like to take over the world, or whatever. The men in charge will assume you have messages in the extra DNA and will not let you free. But if your DNA is the same as your other person's DNA, then it can be used to argue you don't have any more hidden alien messages."

"Okay, so that's good," Patsy said.

"So we test our DNA and our other person's DNA," Sue told the others. "If they match, we're okay. That's easy."

"Yes, but if you don't match and have extra DNA, there will be evidence you have something more, maybe a message."

"Oh, that's not good," Donald said.

"And some DNA tests can be very sensitive. If the analysis shows any difference at all between you and your other person, the officials could say you are different and that would be enough to keep you here forever."

"Then we're not going to do the test," Donald concluded. "We can't take the chance."

"That would be logical," Mary agreed. "But it won't help Ted. If you can't show you don't have any harmful messages, the officials will automatically think you do. Ted may let you go, but the rest of DHS will bring you back."

"Then what do we do?" Martha asked. "I don't want to be brought back."

The other residents all nodded in agreement.

"The best option is a DNA fingerprint test," Mary told them. "They use this test when investigating crimes and when they confirm the parents of children. The analysis doesn't look at the all of a person's DNA. It looks at a few key marker DNA sequences. It's less sensitive, so it can't detect every difference between the DNA of two people. But it can detect when the DNA of one person doesn't match another. If your DNA is the same as your other people's DNA, it will match in the fingerprint test."

"So it is easy after all," Sue remarked.

"Uh… not so fast, Sue. What if the results of the fingerprint show you do not match your other person?"

"Can we hide the results if they don't match?" asked Donald.

"A lab will probably not allow that to happen. They could get in a lot of trouble if someone found out."

"But what if we find the right lab?" Sue asked.

Mary shrugged.

"Can we find the lab in Kansas that Mr. Stevens mentioned?" Sue proposed. "If they know Mr. Stevens and like him, they might help."

Sue was interrupted by the next delivery. A truck pulled up and three men got out. They brought in the laptops and game consoles. Each resident got their own laptop. The delivery men and the staff set up the computers and internet connections. They entered the codes to get access to the Wi-Fi in the Exchange and they were ready to surf. The residents were 'wired' to the internet.

"Where do we start?" wondered Martha.

"Google," Brandy offered. "You can find whatever you want on Google." The other residents crowded around her to see her use the computer. "Just click the blue 'e' with the yellow ring around it. That gets you to the internet. Now type in whatever you want in this space up here where it says 'Google'."

"If I want to find out more about DNA tests, how do I do that?" asked Sue.

"Type 'DNA tests' in Google," Brandy replied.

Sue returned to her chair and started clicking. "Wow. There are lots of things here," Sue noted. "Brandy, what are these blue underlined words?"

"Web pages. Click on the blue words. That's a link to another page. Go ahead… try it."

"Oh! Okay. I see. So all these blue words are links to other screens with more information?"

"Yep."

The younger kids, Larry, Janet, and Martha surfed the

internet randomly. Brandy, Patsy, Donald, and Sue each searched for DNA tests to get more information. After a half hour of surfing and sharing with each other what they found, they had a better understanding of what Mary was saying.

"If we can find the lab where Mr. Stevens had the substance tested originally, we can get blood or hair samples from us and from our other people," Sue proposed. "We can do the DNA fingerprinting using the short tandem repeat test. There is a one in three trillion chance of a random match between two people."

"It's, like, impossible for two different people to match using that test," Patsy added.

"So if our DNA really is the same as our other people's DNA, we'll match. If our results match, we can say that it is not an error. We can say we don't have any extra sequences," Donald summarized.

"So that would mean that we don't have any extra DNA to make us take over the world, right?" Brandy asked.

"We have to find the lab Mr. Stevens went to," Sue insisted. "We have to talk to them. They will know more about this than we do. If we ask Mr. Stevens, do you think he will let us talk to the lab?"

"Ask him," Brandy suggested.

Sue got up and found Ted working in his corner. She asked if she and the others could have a few minutes of his time. He agreed and walked over to the comfy chairs. She invited him to have her chair. He accepted with a smile.

"We'd like to ask you a favor, Mr. Stevens," Sue told him.

"I'm not sure you have many spare favors to use with me, Sue," Ted said slowly shaking his head.

Seeing Ted's reaction, Donald told him, "We want to help you. We want to prove that we are not dangerous to the general public."

"So when you let us go, they won't put you in jail, and they won't come and find us and put *us* back in jail," Sue added.

"What do you have in mind?" Ted asked, definitely curious.

"Sue said you mentioned a message in the DNA in the substance we transformed from," Donald began. "We thought that if there is a message in our DNA, we might be considered dangerous. You know, not human... something different, with extra DNA."

"If our DNA contains more sequences than the people we transformed from, we have extra genetic code, extra messages," Patsy continued.

"But if we don't have extra DNA, we're identical, you know, clones," Brandy added.

"We can argue that we're no more dangerous than our donors, since we're identical," Patsy concluded.

Sue got to the point. "We want to know what lab you went to in Kansas and see if they can do the DNA fingerprint test."

Ted tilted his head and looked at Sue with confusion.

Patsy clarified, "We need a lab that will help you *and* us. We need a lab to do the testing without anyone knowing. If we match, we want to use the test results. But if we are different, we don't want anyone to know the results. If we are different and we do have more DNA than our donors, you and your supervisors will have the data to allow you to keep us here forever. And we'll never be able to leave."

Ted sat for a moment, thinking. "So let me get this straight," he said, rubbing his chin, looking skeptical. "I just can't simply let you go. You think they'll find you and bring you back." After more thought he said, "Yeah, you're probably right. They probably would bring you back and lock the doors once they found out what I did. And they certainly wouldn't be happy with me."

He paused and then confirmed, "So you want to generate DNA fingerprint test results that prove you don't have any dangerous messages in you. If you, the clones, have the same DNA as your other people, you don't have any extra messages. So you're safe. But then if you do the test and you *are* different, you'll be stuck here forever before you even get a chance to leave. Did I get all that correct?"

"Yes," Sue replied.

"So you want to talk to the lab that tested the goo for me previously. And hopefully they can do the fingerprint testing and make bad results go away."

"Yes."

"I see," Ted responded flatly. He stood up and said, "I'll get back with you."

Chapter 31 - Life Saver

Dr. Bailey's cell phone rang. "This is Jim Bailey."

"Jim, it's Ted."

"Are you here again? I'll be right there to let you in."

"No, Jim, I'm in California. Listen, I need to talk to you. Is this a private line? Is anyone else listening?"

"We're okay to talk. No one is listening."

"I had an interesting week, this week, but I won't go into details. I need to ask you a favor. Can you run a couple tests for me?"

"Sure. We're pretty much at DHS's disposal."

"I need you to run a test for *me*, not for DHS. And depending on the results, I need you to record the test or destroy the evidence."

"Uh... I don't know what you're getting at."

"I need to test the clones, the new people. I need to see if their DNA fingerprints match those of their original people. If they match, I need the results. If they don't, we're all in trouble. I don't want to be in trouble, Jim, nor do the clones. I don't want any trace of results that don't match. Can you help me?"

"Uh... it's a tough call, Ted. I'm not even sure it's legal."

"Is it legal to lock up innocent humans on an abandoned

military base for the rest of their lives?"

"Um…"

"It's a tough call, isn't it, Jim?"

The phone line was silent for almost thirty seconds.

"Okay, Ted, here's what you do. Wear disposable gloves when you collect hair samples. Pluck the hairs out so the root is attached. Put the hair in new disposable sterilized bottles with screw caps. You can find those at any drug store. Better yet, get some sterile swabs and swab the inside of people's cheeks too. Make sure you label the bottles with permanent ink so you don't mix up the samples. And make sure everything is as clean as possible. Do not cross-contaminate. And deliver the samples to me in person."

"I'll be in Kansas as soon as I collect samples. I'll keep you posted. You're a life-saver, Jim, literally."

Chapter 32 - I'll be back

At 7:30 the next morning, there was a knock at Sue's front door. Again, it was Ted. She opened the door.

"C'mon, Sue. Come to the Exchange please. I need your DNA." Sue followed blindly and silently without even changing her clothes.

When Sue and Ted arrived at the Exchange, Martha, Janet, Larry, and Patsy were waiting. Mary was also at the exchange. Ted asked her to lock the doors of the Exchange.

When Mary returned, Ted explained the plan. "We're collecting hair samples and cheek swabs to conduct the DNA fingerprint testing. We'll also collect samples from your donors, your other people. The lab has agreed to control the results. We'll know something in a few days. *Do not* tell anyone else about the testing... ever. The less anyone knows, the more protected you will be. It's very important to remember to not tell anyone. Now, let's go sit at the back and we'll take your samples."

"Why are we the only ones giving samples?" Sue asked. "Where's Donald?"

"Donald's other person doesn't know that he has a copy. He doesn't know that a transformation occurred. So he doesn't know he's a donor. The others are children. We would have to get parents' consent to take the samples from the children donors, and they would likely talk... both the kids and their parents. There's way too much chance of word leaking out. Your adult donors, on the other hand, can be convinced it's best to keep quiet."

Sue nodded, understanding the reason.

"Shall we begin?" Ted asked.

Ted put on gloves and plucked a few hairs from Sue's head. He placed the hair in the plastic bottle and screwed on the cap. He also swabbed the inside of her cheek and placed the swab in a separate bottle. He wrote 'SUE2' on the bottles with a black Sharpie pen. He changed his gloves and collected the same hair and swab samples from Martha. He repeated the sampling for Janet, Larry and Patsy. He placed the labeled bottles in zip-lock bags and tossed them all in a large black briefcase, along with the gloves, swabs, empty bottles and the Sharpie. He closed and locked the briefcase.

"I'll be back when I know the results," he told the group. "Until then, please behave." Looking directly at Sue, he added, "And don't leave the base. Thank you."

Chapter 33 - I'm In

Dr. Bailey's cell phone rang. "This is Jim Bailey."

"Jim, it's Ted."

"Are you here?"

"Yes. Can you let me in?"

"I'll be right up."

Jim walked to the front of the building and let Ted in. He escorted Ted to the front conference room where Cindy, Sarah, and Bruno were already sitting. He closed and locked the door. He and Ted sat at the table one on either side of the group leaders.

Ted quietly said, "Sorry for getting so close, but I need to talk softly. Jim told me that he gave you all a head's up. Is that right?"

The group leaders nodded.

"I need to know right now if you're prepared to do what Jim and I ask, no matter what it is. Can we rely on you?"

The group leaders nodded again.

"Good. I have samples which I need tested. But I only want the results if they show one thing. If they show something else, I don't want anyone to see the results or any trace of the testing... *ever.*"

The group leaders looked nervously at their boss. Jim

nodded to reassure them.

Ted continued, "I have hair and swab samples from the adults who transformed from the goo. And I have hair and swab samples from the adults who touched the goo. I want to see if the clones match the donors. I want to get a DNA fingerprint test. If the donors match the clones, I want the results. If they don't match, I don't want anyone to know. I want the test results destroyed."

The group leaders looked again to Dr. Bailey for reassurance. Jim nodded again.

"Here's the deal," Ted explained, "I can't keep the clones locked up. They cannot live forever isolated on a military base. So I'm going to let them go. But as soon as I do, DHS will lock me up. And they'll find the clones and lock them up too. They can't win. Unless we prove to DHS there is no hidden programming that's going to turn these people into crazed aliens that will take over the world. If we can show the clones are true clones... if we can show they are identical to their donors, we can say they're no different from the donors, all of whom are normal, law-abiding, Earth-loving citizens. Are you with me so far?"

The group leaders silently nodded.

"If the results don't show the clones are identical and there actually is extra genetic programming in the clones, no one can know it. Otherwise they'll be locked up forever... or worse."

The group leaders sat and thought for a minute.

"How do we do it?" Cindy asked Jim.

"We'll start new notebooks," Jim instructed. "All reagents will be prepared for these tests only, and then destroyed after. Only make reference to equipment logs or SOPs as needed. And nothing external will reference these special notebooks. Document everything in these notebooks only. Record analyst work hours to our general DHS project code... nothing more specific than that. Keep it neat and clean in case it all has to go away."

"What if DHS finds out?" Sarah asked. "We could lose

our jobs."

"Yes," Jim confirmed, "we'd lose our jobs."

Seeing that Jim's response didn't go over well with the group leaders, Ted leaned in close, made eye contact with each group leader, and added his own response, "I *am* losing my job. As soon as they find out I even considered letting these people go, I'm done. So when I *do* let them go, I'll never work another day in my life. I just hope I don't go to prison. But I can't keep these people locked up. They have done nothing wrong. They're delivering a message. That's it."

"Delivering a message?" Bruno asked.

"Did I not tell you? One of our residents escaped from the base. She returned to her original house, to her donor's house. She told them why the pods and substance are here on Earth. They were sent to deliver a message about an extinct species from a planet that died a long time ago. She didn't know much else… maybe more details will come to light in the future. But she did know the pods were sent out so the species would not die unnoticed." He stopped to let the analysts process what he told them. Then he added, "After delivering her message to her 'family', she willingly let me take her back to her house on the base."

"I'm in," Cindy declared.

"Same here," Sarah agreed.

"Me too," Bruno said.

"Thank you. I thank you all. And the residents thank you, too."

Chapter 34 - Waiting

Several days passed without any word from Ted.   The staff knew nothing and the residents knew less. They had spent almost every waking hour together in the café, eating meals, drinking coffee, surfing the internet, and waiting under a cloud of tension, wondering.

The counselors moved a TV into the Exchange so the kids could play video games during the day and be in the company of the adults. Everyone at the base had become a little closer since Ted announced they'd be leaving.

Sue spent as much time with the kids as she did with the adults.   Kati and Violet were her new friends.   To the children, Sue was like a mother. She cooked for them (and for the adults, of course) and taught them.   She played games with them but still nagged at them when they complained about her dinners. Sue refused to make frozen pizza or burgers every night as they requested, and made them eat vegetables. She helped them read books and use their computers. The children, especially Kati and Violet, reminded Sue of Karen. Sue missed Karen.

During the afternoon espresso hour, a week after Ted left, the usual activities were interrupted. Ted returned. He entered the Exchange and walked back to the café, plopped his briefcase in a chair, opened it, and pulled out two research notebooks. "Your DNA matches your other people's DNA. No difference."

Cheers filled the Exchange. Residents and staff danced with each other in excitement. Everyone came up to Ted to thank him and shake his hand. He smiled. He was equally thankful to them for suggesting the solution and supporting him. But more than anything, he was relieved the results supported his decision.

When the celebration ebbed a bit, Ted was forced to interrupt and get down to business. "Okay, okay... settle down for a couple minutes, please. We have several details to go though, so I need your attention."

Everyone took a seat and listened.

"Thank you. We can celebrate all night after we take care of some business. You are all free to leave, but first I have to talk to DHS. I have to convince them to not bring you back. The fingerprint data will help. I also need to make arrangements for you. So I need each of the adults to think about where you want to live and what you want to do. I need to know by tomorrow morning, so you have until breakfast tomorrow to tell me." He paused to let his instructions sink in with the residents.

"Now, the kids... We don't have a lot of options here. I need everyone's help for ideas. We can find foster homes for these kids, but that's a lot of red tape to go through. We could take them back to their donors' families..." He thought about the option for a moment as he said it, but then shook his head. "No, that would be too much for them to deal with. What other options do we have?"

"We can't put them in foster homes," Juliana replied. They need dedicated parenting. And what would we tell the foster parents? How would we explain these kids' history?"

"Can we keep them here, like a camp?" TJ asked.

"Without school?" Denise asked. "Stuck here? How would they fit into society if they never went to any school? Brandy is already socially behind. She should be getting ready for high school, you know... listening to music, texting her friends, talking non-stop on the phone, and dating boys."

No one responded right away, but they all knew that Denise was right.

"Can the adults adopt them?" Juliana wondered.

"That's a great idea!" Sue agreed.

Thinking carefully as he talked, Ted replied, "I don't... well, it would be easier to have you all be their parents. That's a lot less explaining we have to do. But do you want to include children in your new lives? You all are very lucky. You get to choose your life. You get to choose what you want to do. Do you want to start out with children right away? This is a huge decision."

"Maybe," Martha responded, "but we can't just leave them alone because we don't want to take care of them. We can't abandon them."

"I want to adopt them," Sue insisted.

"You cannot adopt all five children, Sue," Ted countered tersely, shutting off discussion. He sighed. "Before we go any further, I want you all to sit by yourselves and decide what you want to do. You can ask the staff what they think. But I want your decisions to be your own. I don't want anyone else to influence you."

The clones nodded at Ted.

"So sit, think, and decide. I have a lot of phone calls to make. I must leave now, but I'll be back tomorrow morning. Goodbye all."

Chapter 35 - Decisions

They had their instructions from Ted, but no one really knew where to start.

Mary gave them some ideas to focus their thoughts. "Think about what you like to do. Think about what you're interested in. Think about what you can do, what skills you have. I know you're supposed to do this by yourselves, but let me see if I can give you an example. Sue likes to cook. She might like to cook for a job."

"I already cooked for a job, at the truck stop," Sue replied.

"So a job as a cook is a good job for Sue," Mary told the others. "But we can't just find her a job in a high class restaurant in New York City. She's not properly trained for that job. She could work at McDonalds, but they don't really cook. I think Sue might have found her perfect job at that truck stop as a short-order cook."

"And someone here likes to make coffee, but I can't remember who it is," Juliana said sarcastically.

"Me!"

"Oh yeah, Martha!" Juliana smiled. "She might be a really good barista at a coffee shop."

"I'd like that!"

"Donald, do you have any ideas?" Mary asked.

"I don't really have any desires like Sue or Martha. I enjoy reading and learning and talking with people. I like to help out."

"You could write helpful books," Patsy suggested.

"I don't think he's ready for that just yet, Patsy, but something along those lines may be a good fit," Denise replied. Turning to Donald, she asked, "What if you start as an employee in a book store, Donald? You can help people find good books and talk with them. And you can read books on your off hours. There are a huge number of books in a store."

"That sounds like a good start," Donald agreed. "I'd like to give more help though."

"With time you will," Denise reassured him.

"I worked on a farm. I could go back to doing that," Larry proposed.

"I'd like to go to college and get a degree," Patsy told the others.

"These are all great ideas," Mary responded. "I think you all are off to a good start. Sit by yourselves and write. Use your computers to look up things on the internet. Write down what you want to do, where you want to live, what would make you happy. By dinner, if you all have ideas, we can share them. How does that sound?"

They residents all agreed.

The counselors took the kids back to the cabins to play games since the children weren't able to make their own decisions. And the counselors didn't want the children to interrupt the adults.

The adults sat in the comfy chairs, each focusing on their assignment. The afternoon at the Exchange passed in near silence.

As the sun started to set, everyone began to stir. They had thought for a long time and their brains were getting tired. They were also hungry.

No one noticed Denise and Juliana sneak out of the

exchange earlier, but they all noticed when they returned with pizza and soda for all.

The counselors returned to the Exchange, along with the kids, and after everyone got food and drink, Mary kicked off a review of the residents' decisions. "So, did you get very far with your choices?"

"I did," Sue boasted. "Am I allowed to tell you guys?"

"I think so," Mary replied.

"I want to move back to Kansas and be a cook in a diner. I want to cook for the people in Enterprise. I even found a restaurant where I can work. I found it on the internet. And I want to have a family. And I want to be close to Karen. She's like my sister. I don't think the other Sue will mind. I couldn't find a house. I hope Ted can find one for me."

Thank you, Sue," Mary responded. "I hope we can make all that come true for you."

"Anyone want to guess what Martha wants to do?" Juliana asked. "I bet you can't guess."

"Duh! Barista! I'm gonna be a Barista," Martha proudly announced. "I read about all the things I can make at a coffee shop."

"Yes, but where will you live?"

"I like it here… wherever we are," Martha replied. "It's warm. But it doesn't feel hot. I like the warm days and the cool nights."

"We're in the desert, the Southwest," Juliana told her. "So you probably want to settle in Arizona, California, or Nevada. Are you okay living by yourself?"

"I guess… unless anyone wants to live with me. Anyone want to live with me?"

"Sorry, Martha," Sue responded. "I'll be in Kansas."

"Not me. I think I'd like to work on a farm back in Wisconsin," Larry suggested.

"You know, they do have dairy cows in California also," Carl informed Larry. "More cows than in Wisconsin."

"Yeah, I read that on the internet. But I also read on the internet that most farms in California are big farms. I liked working on a small farm in Wisconsin. I hope I can find one."

"I wouldn't mind living out here in the Southwest," Patsy said to the group. "I'd like to go to college. Maybe I could go to college in the same city as Martha."

"Patsy, do you think you have enough knowledge to go to college?" Juliana asked. "Most kids go to school for 12 years before college. You're the right age for college, but I'm not sure you could get a good score on an aptitude... a college entrance exam."

"I don't know. I guess I don't have the right knowledge. What do I have to do?"

"Get your high school diploma," Denise told Patsy. "You could go to high school, but you're a little old. You can get a high school equivalency degree by passing the GED test. You can work during the day and study at night to prepare for the test."

"You and Martha could both work during the day, making coffee," Juliana suggested.

"That sounds good to me. Then neither of us would be alone. What do you think Martha? Can I be your roommate?"

"Yeah! That sounds good!" Martha agreed. Let's do that!"

"Janet," Mary asked, "what do you think you want to do?"

"I don't know. I don't really have anything I can do."

"Is there anything you'd like to do? Is there anything that makes you happy?"

"Maybe go back to Wisconsin. Maybe I can be trained to do something."

Trying to make sure no one would live unsupervised or alone, Mary made a suggestion. "Larry, what would you think about living near Janet so you can help each other? Would that be okay with you?"

"I think so... yeah. I think I could do that. Janet, would you like that?"

"Are you proposing to me Larry?" Janet giggled.

"Er…"

"I'd love it, Larry! I accept."

Larry was a little embarrassed, but didn't try to retract his offer.

With the awkward break in the conversation, Carl suggested the counselors and children retire for the evening to one of the cabins to watch a movie or play games while the adults had coffee and continued talking.

Taking the cue from Carl, the counselors rounded up the kids and headed out of the Exchange.

When he saw they had crossed Main Street, Carl continued the discussion. "Now, we want to ask for your opinions about the children. We don't know what is possible, but we think you all should have your say."

Sue, as usual, was the first to respond. "They have to be treated well. You cannot put them with other families that don't know them."

"If we don't put them in foster homes, they will have to move with you," Carl told her. "Or we'll have to move them to someone who knows about their situation."

"I agree with Sue," Donald said. "They can't move with people who don't want them."

"They can move with me to Kansas," Sue suggested.

"Like Ted said earlier, you cannot take care of five children," Denise responded.

"I can too. I can cook. I can clean. I can read with them and watch TV and--"

"Sue, we know you can do all that, but not for *five* children," Denise told her. "It's much more difficult than you realize. It's hard raising just one child. Five is really *really* difficult. You have to trust us."

"Well, what about Kati and Violet? I can raise two children."

Mary chimed in, "This is a big responsibility Sue. If you agree to take care of these kids, you can't give them back. They are your responsibility forever."

"I know. I saw the other Sue and Karen together. I saw Petunia take care of Karen too. I played with Karen. I read with her. I couldn't cook for her because I didn't know how. But now I can. I know I can take care of Kati and Violet. I'll be the best mommy, I promise."

"We'll talk to Mr. Stevens tomorrow," Mary told her. "What about the other children? Anyone have any thoughts?"

No one responded. None of the other adults was ready to commit to becoming a parent. And after observing these six adults for a while, the staff knew that only Sue had any real potential for being a parent on her own.

"Okay. Think about some ideas," Carl instructed. "They don't have to be final options. But we need to give Ted some ideas tomorrow when he arrives." He paused to see each resident's agreement. "I need to turn in for the night. I think Denise agreed to help close up tonight, correct?"

"Yep, I did."

"I'll help Denise," Juliana added. "Thanks Carl. Goodnight."

"Goodnight then," Carl said to all. "Sleep well. We'll see each other in the morning."

Mary followed Carl's lead by standing and saying, "I'll take this opportunity to leave as well. Goodnight."

She and Carl left the Exchange.

"Martha," Denise called out, "Do we need some coffee? Maybe an espresso?"

"I don't know, do we?"

"I'd like an espresso," Denise said.

"Me too," added Donald.

"Regular coffee for me please, roommate!" Patsy smiled.

"Nothing for me, thanks," Sue replied.

"Me either," Janet said.

"Not me," Larry added. "I'm good."

"I'll help Martha," Juliana volunteered. "This may be one of the last times we can make coffee together."

Martha and Juliana stood up to start making coffee

together. As they walked to the coffee maker, Martha asked Juliana, "Do you think Mr. Stevens will let me have the coffee maker?"

Laughing and smiling, Juliana replied, "I think you've earned it. Besides, you're the only one who really knows how to use it."

After coffee was served, Donald started a new conversation, "Denise, what will you do when we leave?"

"I'll go back to my previous life."

"What was that?" he asked. "What did you do?"

"I was an assistant in a branch office of the department, Homeland Security. I processed intelligence information we collected from all over the world. It wasn't very exciting, or not as exciting as you might think. I used to be a YMCA camp director before that. They knew I had experience with situations that might be similar to what we were expecting here at the base. And they knew I could handle confidential information. I already had the security clearance."

"What about you Juliana?" Janet called over to the coffee maker.

"I was a psychology major in college," Juliana replied. "I was in training to administer tests to witnesses, you know, lie-detector tests, psychological screenings, and stuff like that."

"So what will you do when we leave?" Donald asked.

"I guess I'll go back to my old job," Juliana replied. "But that'll be boring compared to these weeks with you guys."

"Yeah, it will," agreed Denise.

"You obviously don't have families, do you?" Sue deduced.

"How did you come to that conclusion?" Denise asked.

"Am I right?"

"Well, yeah. But how did you know?"

"Mr. Stevens wouldn't pull people away from their families to watch us," Sue concluded.

"Ted might not, but the government would," Juliana responded. "If they need you and you work for them, they'll pretty much make you do what they want. We have jobs that have good benefits, but they can make it difficult if they need to."

"Is the Department of Homeland Security a good part of the government?" asked Donald.

"It's the biggest," Denise replied. "There are a lot of people in it. And not everyone is fighting terror and being spies and stuff. Most people in the department just try to keep it from collapsing on itself. For most of us, it's a steady job. Unless you really screw up, it's guaranteed employment for those of us little people."

"Can I get a job in the department?" Donald inquired.

"Maybe, I guess, but why would you want to?" Juliana asked. "A government job isn't very glamorous or rewarding. You basically go unnoticed, unless you screw up, like Denise said. Then you get bad assignments that no one ever wants."

"I don't know why I would want to," Donald answered. "I like you two and I like Mr. Stevens. You seem to be good people to work with."

"You probably can get a job in the department if you really want to," Denise responded. "It's the government, not the general public, so we can probably find a position for you. And I'm sure there's a job you can do. But you can find a job almost anywhere with nice people to work with, Donald. We're not the only nice people. But, if you're really interested, you can tell Ted about it tomorrow."

"Okay, I will."

"I can't wait to tell Mr. Stevens what I want to do," Sue jumped in. "I hope I can do what I want. I hope he'll let me cook in Enterprise and take care of Kati and Violet. I really want to do that. I don't know if I can wait until tomorrow morning. Good thing I didn't have any coffee. I'd never get to sleep." She yawned and then stood up out of her comfy chair to leave. "I think I'll go home a read a book to fall asleep."

"I think I'll turn in too," Larry added, as he also stood up to leave.

"Me too, I'm tired," Janet agreed. She joined the other two.

Holding his arms out to take the arms of Sue and Janet, Larry asked, "Shall we, ladies?"

"Larry! You proposed to *me*. You can't walk another woman home!" Janet joked.

The three exited the Exchange together. They walked across Main Street. Sue reached her house first and left the other two. Janet and Larry continued walking together toward their houses.

The others sipped the last of their coffees in the Exchange café.

"What should I study if I go to college?" Patsy asked the group.

"You can study whatever you want, whatever you're good at," Denise replied.

"What are you good at, Patsy?" Martha asked.

"I don't know."

"Then you have a lot of options," Juliana concluded. "You can figure out what you should study in college when you complete your high school degree. You'll find something."

"Maybe I'll study science. I liked learning all the stuff about DNA. Or maybe math... or... ah, you're right. I have plenty of time to figure it out." Patsy continued, "I hope we can find a cool place to live, Martha, maybe close to a college. College kids are fun. And, they drink lots of coffee. So we can find jobs. There will be lots of coffee shops near a college."

"I can't wait!" Martha said.

Trying to wrap things up so they could all get some sleep, Juliana asked, "So... are we all ready to call it a night?"

"Yeah, I guess so," Patsy answered.

"Yes. I'm tired. This has been a busy day," Martha responded.

"And a long day," Donald added.

"Let's close up. I'll get the lights, Juliana. I have Donald to protect me," Denise smiled. "You can drop Martha and Patsy off."

"That sounds good," Juliana replied. She called to Patsy and Martha, "C'mon you two. Let's get you back home. We've got another big day tomorrow." She held the door for Martha and Patsy. They left the Exchange and happily walked toward the houses, arm-in-arm. Each was excited about the next day.

Denise turned the off lights in the café, and then walked to the entrance with Donald. She flipped the switches to turn off the remaining lights. The only source of light remaining was the street light outside the Exchange. Donald held the door open for her and they walked out. Denise locked the door. "I don't know why we have to lock this silly door," she said. "I guess we thought we had to originally. Now we don't need to, but… I guess I better lock it. Ted wouldn't be happy if I didn't. So there, I locked it." She rolled her eyes and shook her head. "Oh, would you listen to me babble?"

Donald held his arm out for Denise. She took it and they walked toward the houses, into the dark, away from the street light.

Chapter 36 - Uncle Ted

No one needed to knock on anyone's door to wake them the next morning. After hearing the jet land at the base, everyone was awake, waiting for the black sedan to pull up to the Exchange. The man in the black suit with the black portfolio barely got out of the car before the residents swarmed him with chatter. "Okay, okay! Let's at least get inside," Ted called out. "I'll listen to each of you in there."

Everyone followed Ted into the Exchange and stood around him waiting for his instructions. "Please. Sit down. Relax. Have some coffee. Go... all of you." He shooed them to the café with his hands. "I'll be with you shortly."

Martha was the first to the café to make coffee. The others filtered back to take seats in the comfy chairs.

Ted called out a request, "May I have a word with the staff for a few minutes?"

The staff members rolled their eyes and sighed. *Why couldn't he have told us to join him before we sat down?* They reluctantly got out of their seats and slowly returned to the front of the Exchange.

When the staff finally assembled, Ted asked, "Did you get an idea of what we might have to arrange?"

"The usual kinds of things for relocations... IDs, houses,

jobs," Carl replied.

"We may have a problem," Mary informed Ted.

"Which is?"

"Three of the kids," Mary replied. "No one volunteered. Sue would like to adopt Kati and Violet. But that's it."

"Maybe not," Denise interjected. "Donald said some things last night. Let's hear what he has to say."

Ted looked at her with a raised eyebrow. He wondered what that meant. Turning to the others, he asked, "Anything else?"

"Not really," replied Carl. "This should be a relatively straightforward relocation. The children will be the trickiest part."

"Okay, let's go."

Ted and the staff walked back to the café. All but Ted took a seat.

"Okay," Ted began. "Ready? This is your chance to pick your future. What will it be?" he asked, looking to the clones. "Sue, you look like you're having trouble staying seated. You can go first."

"I want to go back to Enterprise and work in a diner and make food for people and be close to Karen and have Kati and Violet live with me. I asked them. They like the idea."

"Okay. Thank you, Sue." He paused a moment and then said, "Now, I have a couple questions for you. One, if you live in Enterprise where Susan, the original Sue lives, will you also be named Susan Roberts?"

"Can I?"

"Don't you think the people of Enterprise might get confused if there are two Susan Roberts in town who look like they're twins?" Ted watched Sue think for a bit, and then continued, "What about a new name, maybe Suzanne?"

"That makes sense. I guess I could be Suzanne. Suzanne Roberts."

"Er... you probably have to change your last name also. You need to be the new person in town. Someone not associated with Susan Roberts."

"What about Suzanne Cook?" Denise suggested.

"Yeah, I like that! I'll be Suzanne Cook."

"Good. Now, second, why are you going to be a good mother for Kati and Violet?"

"Because I like them, just like I like Karen. I've seen how to take care of Karen. I watched the other Sue and Petunia. I want to teach them and cook for them."

"What can you teach Kati and Violet? You have the same knowledge as a normal eight year old child."

"Maybe more!" Sue protested. "I've read a lot. And I've been surfing."

"Agreed, but how are you going to teach them as they grow to adults when you don't have an adult's level of knowledge?"

"I'll learn too. I will learn as they learn. We'll learn together," Sue proposed.

"You need someone to help you," Ted informed her. "You need someone or some people to be there to help you if you need it."

"Okay," Sue reluctantly replied.

Ted proactively raised his hands to calm her before continuing, "You'll be a mother for life. You can't give them to anyone to take care of."

"I will *not* give them to anyone!" Sue snapped.

Ted looked at her, waiting for her next proposal.

She thought about options for future assistance, and then replied, "Maybe Petunia can help me, but only when I need it."

"Are you sure you want to be the parent for the girls? Are you absolutely sure?"

"Yes, I'm absolutely sure."

Ted paused to consider Sue's response before making his decision. He looked into Sue's eyes and replied, "Okay." Turning to the other clones, he said, "So, that's it for Sue… er… Suzanne. Who's next?"

"Me!" Martha jumped in. "I'm next. I want to live near a college in the Southwest and work in a coffee shop. Patsy has agreed to share a house with me. She'll study at night, and then go to the college when she passes the GED test. She'll meet people her age at the coffee shop where we'll work during the day." She paused and turned to Pasty, "Oh, sorry Patsy. I spoke for you."

"No problem, Martha. You got it right."

"Okay, thank you Martha and Patsy." Ted reviewed their proposal, "No original town or name issues... you'll both help each other... no kids... Martha will get to make coffee..." He smiled at Martha and then Patsy. "Yes, I think that will work for you two. Who's next?"

Larry made his proposal. "Janet and I would like to settle in Wisconsin. I liked working on the farm. We could find another farm for me to work on. Janet can work in a shop or something. We can help each other. I'd be glad to help Janet."

"Okay," Ted said cautiously. "That sounds good. However... finding a farm that is hiring a farmhand might be tough. But we'll give it a try. And you two will be okay together?" Ted asked, looking at Janet.

"Yes. Larry is a good man."

Larry added, "I'll take care of her, Mr. Stevens. I promise."

"Good. I wish you good luck in your new homes in Wisconsin. Okay, next... Donald?"

Donald looked at Denise and then blushed. He turned to Ted and replied, "Denise and I have decided we'd like to be together."

Gasps fill the room, followed by squeals, laughing, and congratulations.

When the excitement waned, Donald explained to all, "We've kind of known for a while that we were... interested in each other. But we never talked about anything because we didn't know there was a future. But now that there will be, we decided to talk about it. Turns out, we have a lot of the same ideas."

"I can go back to my old job," Denise added, looking at

Ted. "Maybe we can get Donald a job there. I'll tell everyone he was working at this assignment when I met him."

"How convenient," Ted replied, smiling broadly. "We'll have to see what we can do for you two. Again, congratulations. Next--"

"Wait," Denise said. She looked to Donald and then to Brandy. "We'd like to adopt Brandy if she'd like that. She needs to have people around her that understand her. Donald and I would like to be those people."

More gasps fill the room. Everyone looked to Brandy, who looked at Donald and Denise. Her eyes lit up and she smiled. She was about to respond, when Ted started to talk.

"I think that sounds like a good idea," Ted said, "but before we determine the children's fate, I need to talk with them. I'd like to have a few minutes alone with them. Can you adults all excuse me and let me talk to these special people? Thank you."

The adults looked silently at each other, asking if Ted was serious. Deciding he was, they stood and walked over to the shelves of items in the front of the Exchange, leaving Ted with the kids.

"Okay," Ted began, addressing the children. "I need to talk to you five."

The children looked to each other for support. They weren't sure why Ted had isolated them without the other residents or the counselors.

Ted got down on one knee to be at their eye level. He smiled at each of them reassuringly, and told them, "We've been talking to the adults for all this time, because they have ideas about what they want to do. And since they're adults, they get to choose. I will help them with their choices, but they get to pick. Children, on the other hand, don't always get what they want in our society. But you five are not ordinary kids. We all know you're special kids. So I want to hear what you want. I have to make sure you'll be happy. And I have to make sure you'll be taken care of." Turning to the youngest girls, he said, "Kati and Violet... Sue has requested that you live with her. She would be your mother. What do you think about that?"

"I like Sue," Kati replied, looking directly at Ted. "She likes to read with us and teach us. But she's not very good at video games."

"Does she need to be good at video games to be a good mother?"

"No," Kati said, smiling. "I like it that we can beat her."

"Do you think that Sue will be a good mother, not just a teacher or friend?"

"Yes," Violet declared.

"What makes you say that for sure, Violet?"

"She has fun with us. She teaches us."

"What happens if you get sick? If you get sick and can't go to school, what will she do for you?"

"I don't know. Maybe hold my hand. She'll try to make me better."

"I think she'll feed me," offered Kati. "Maybe she'll get a nurse, like Mary."

"What happens if you two break one of her coffee cups or a plate from her kitchen? What do you think she will do?"

"She would *not* be happy," Kati said. "She likes her kitchen dishes."

"She might tell us we're messy. Or... she might even make us clean it up," Violet suggested.

Ted grinned at their responses. Satisfied, Ted said, "Okay. Thank you, ladies. I wish you and your mother good luck." He smiled at the girls. "Now, Brandy... Donald and Denise would like to adopt you. I know Denise will be a good mother. And Donald will be a really good father. But what do you think about them?"

"I guess they'll be okay," Brandy answered. "I mean... I like Denise and Donald a lot. And they like me. All I know is how bad the other Brandy's parents were. Compared to them, Denise and Donald will be better... *a lot* better."

"Do you think they'll give you what you need as you

grow older to an adult?"

"I don't know what I will need."

"Exactly. Will Denise know what you will need?"

"Uh, yah! She knows what everyone needs. And Donald will be good at helping her."

Ted had the utmost confidence in Denise, and was confident that Donald would be a good husband for Denise. "Will you agree to have Denise and Donald be your parents? Or shall I call them guardians?"

"I'm good with them being my parents."

"Okay. I wish you the best." He smiled at Brandy who smiled back.

"Now for you two gentlemen…" Ted turned to the boys, and gave them a smile. He tried to provide an air of confidence. "Let's think about a family for you."

"I like TJ!" Tyler suggested.

"So do I," Zachary agreed.

"TJ is too young to be a parent," Ted replied.

"What about Donald and Denise?" Tyler asked.

"They'll have Brandy," Ted said. "I think that's enough for them."

"What about you?" Zachary asked.

"No, boys," he told them with a quick laugh, "I would not be a good father. I'm always traveling, so I'm often not at home. But I'll still visit you, I promise. I'll be more like an uncle."

"Uncle Ted!" Zachary announced.

"I like that!" Tyler agreed. "Uncle Ted!"

"I have someone in mind for you two boys. I can't say anything right now until I confirm a few things. But don't worry… we'll find you two a good home living together with people who care about you very much. That's my promise to you."

Tyler and Zachary smiled at Ted.

Looking to all of the children, Ted asked, "Are you all excited to be leaving here and going to new homes?"

They nodded and voiced their agreement.

"I know this whole thing has been difficult for you all, having to move several times and being here at this camp. But you have all done well and learned a lot. I will be very happy to watch you all grow up."

Ted looked up to find where the adults were. He found them scattered near the front of the Exchange and called them all back to the café.

When they all sat down in the comfy chairs, Ted summarized. "Okay. I have all of your requests and will begin to make arrangements. I'll be back as soon as I can with an update. Expect me in three to four days. I'll have final details and documents." He was about to turn to leave when he stopped and slapped his forehead. "I almost forgot. I need your pictures. Okay, everyone line up." He motioned the adults into a spot by the wall of the Exchange. "Now, where did I put that camera... ah, here it is! Okay, I need each of your pictures, one at a time."

Ted proceeded to take several pictures of each resident using a digital camera. When finished, he pushed several buttons and then removed a memory card from the camera.

Motioning all back to the chairs, he continued giving instructions. "Now... I'll be back, like I said, in three to four days with final details and documents. I will also meet with the Department. That's when I'll give them the results of the DNA testing." He paused and smiled at all. "And now I must be leaving. I have a lot of work to do. Stay well... keep learning... and keep drinking coffee!" He turned to walk out and said, "Goodbye all!"

Everyone waved as Ted departed the Exchange. The staff and residents all excitedly shared thoughts about their future. They each congratulated Denise and Donald, sometimes more than once. And Sue started taking orders for a late breakfast.

Chapter 37 - Passing Through

Four days later, Ted returned to the Exchange. He arrived at 7:00 in the morning and, as usual with his visits, the residents and staff were awake and waiting at the Exchange.

He carried a large briefcase which he handed to Carl as they all entered the Exchange and assembled in the café. Ted began, "I cannot stay long. So I have to make this quick. First, today is moving day!"

Everyone cheered.

"I have given details to Carl and he can give them you. I'm just passing through on my way to meet with the Department. But I wanted to talk to you in person. All the arrangements have been made. I'll review them in a minute. Like I said, Carl will give you additional details. It is very important that you understand a few things. I will meet with the Department at two o'clock this afternoon in Washington, that's eleven o'clock here. Around that time, a plane will arrive. That's the plane that will take you to your new homes. Carl, Mary, Juliana, and Denise will go with all of you on the plane. You will say goodbye to the counselors. They won't be traveling with you.

"Okay, second... what to bring. Make sure you take your

computers and any clothes, books, or DVDs you want. Anything in the Exchange can go with you as long as you can carry it. Please don't try to take the frozen or refrigerated food. Or the new chairs." He smiled at everyone.

"Next, your itinerary... Martha and Patsy will be moving to Tempe Arizona near the campus of Arizona State University. You will both work in a coffee shop on campus, Cupz, spelled with a zee. You start working in two days. I have arranged for GED study materials for Patsy. You two will be roommates in a two-bedroom apartment. Juliana will get you two settled in and stay with you about a week. It is hot in Arizona, so stay cool.

"Oh yeah... I almost forgot. Everyone please listen. This is important. All of you have to stay out of the sun. If you are repeatedly exposed to the sun without sunscreen or hats or clothes on, you will damage your cells. Make sure you always wear shirts and hats and put on a lot of sunscreen, SPF-fifty. And no sunbathing! It's *very important*." He waited to see all of the clones nod in response.

"Okay, next: Kansas. Sue... er, sorry... Suzanne, Kati, Violet, Tyler, and Zachary will get off in Kansas. Sue and the girls will have a house in Enterprise." Speaking quietly to Carl, he commented, "It's amazing how local zoning laws can be bent for DHS." Ted continued speaking to the group, "There is also a new home for the boys in the same town. You'll get more details later. Sue, you have a job at the Smokey Hill Café in Enterprise. They recently lost their breakfast cook. I told them I had the perfect replacement." Smiling to Sue, he added, "Don't let me down."

"I won't," Sue replied.

Ted continued, "Denise, Donald, and Brandy will be with you for a few days to get you settled in Enterprise. And that leaves Wisconsin. Janet and Larry, you will be accompanied by Carl and Mary. They will get you settled in your home in Spring Green. Larry, I found a diary farm for you to work. The owner is happy to have another farmhand. And I have found a cheese factory for you Janet. It's down the road in Arena, Wisconsin. They make and sell their own cheese. Carl will stay for a few days. Mary is planning on staying longer. She said she might just retire in Wisconsin." Ted smiled and Mary. Janet and Larry did too. "You two will need to learn to drive a car. So that's something you need to plan to do right away. Mary agreed to help teach you to drive."

Ted paused to take a breath. "Okay, I think that's it. Again, Carl has more details. I have to leave now. I will call when the committee meeting is over." He turned and started walking toward the doors. "And I will see you all in your new homes! Goodbye and good luck!"

As he hurried out of the Exchange, everyone waved and said goodbye. The residents turned their attention to moving. Sue didn't bother with making breakfast. Martha didn't make any coffee. The residents were too excited and had too many things to do before their plane took off.

The staff watched the black sedan drive off. Their thoughts were with Ted and what he was about to face.

Chapter 38 - Green Light

"This meeting was a little rushed, Ted," General Gilmore said. "What's the urgency? Is everything under control?"

"Yes sir. It's all good," Ted started. "You all received my report regarding the resident who escaped the base. Her disappearance revealed several findings. I want to elaborate on the content of that report and give you some new information in person. I hope that's okay with this committee."

"Fire away, Ted," the Chairman responded, leaning back in his chair, relaxed.

"In my report I presented what the resident said to her original family when she returned to Kansas. She indicated that the pods of substance were sent from another planet. From a planet that had died. She told them the alien species on that planet had died and the memory of that species cannot die. When I arrived in Kansas, I safely escorted her back to the base. Nothing dangerous happened. Now... what I didn't get into in the report is the substance that showed up around the country, sent in the ceramic eggs and gelatin pods, had some sort of genetic code. Presumably it's the message that the resident delivered. The transformed humans were able to decipher the message. We assume that lower animal species are not able to decipher or cannot communicate the message."

Mr. Mason raised an eyebrow and asked, "How did you know there's a message in the substance?"

"I didn't. And neither did the lab. We know there's genetic material in the substance, but it's so complex it couldn't be deciphered. The genetic material in the substance is not the same as human DNA, it's much more complex. The message must have been buried somewhere in the goo."

"What does that DNA, the alien DNA do?" Mr. Mason continued probing.

"It's hard to know for sure. The lab tried to sequence it, but there's too much. It's probably what triggers the transformation from substance to animal, or human."

"What else is in the substance? What other messages are we going to receive one day?" General Gilmore asked, sitting up in his chair.

"We don't know. As I said, it's too complex to decipher. The transformed humans are the only ones that can figure it out. And they don't know. As far as anyone knows they're normal people who have an idea or a memory about a species that died a long time ago, a long way away."

"Normal people? Are you trying to tell me you consider these aliens to be normal people?" Mr. Wright challenged. "Are you nuts?"

"No. I'm not crazy," Ted replied bluntly. "And to answer your question, yes, these are normal people. That's the new information I'm here to present." He pulled out the notebooks from Dr. Bailey's lab. "I have here, in these notebooks, DNA fingerprint testing results. We wondered the same as you're wondering right now. We took samples from the residents and their donors, the original people who touched the goo from which the residents transformed. We tested their DNA fingerprints. We compared the residents, the clones, to their donors. You see, with the fingerprint test there is a one in three trillion chance of two random people having the same DNA fingerprint. That's essentially a zero percent chance of two people having the same fingerprint. There would have to be five hundred times as many people on the planet... *five hundred times* more people on Earth before two people would randomly match." Ted paused to see if the numbers and probabilities were sinking in with the committee. Assuming they got it, he continued, "The clones' DNA fingerprints exactly match those from their donors."

"So... that means?" Mr. Wright asked.

"So they, the clones, the people at the base do not have any difference in their genetic material compared to their normal human donors. They are exact copies."

"We're not following you, Ted," the chairman said.

"The residents are identical to the original humans. There is no difference between the people at the base and those living free in the general public."

"Where are you going with this, Ted?" the general asked, nervously shifting in his chair.

"The residents do not pose any threat. There are no hidden genetic messages in these people. There is nothing to trigger any alien attack or any sort of hostile action like that. These are normal people."

"And...?"

Ted paused and took a deep breath for courage. "I'm releasing them. I'm letting them go."

"YOU'RE WHAT?"

"I'm letting them go. I'm relocating the residents."

"You're letting the aliens go? You can't do that!" the general shouted, standing up out of his chair.

"They are *not* aliens!" Ted replied. "They're humans. You can't tell the difference. And yes, I can let these people go. I was given the assignment to contain the situation. And I did. We housed these people long enough to determine the full extent of the situation. They are not going to attack the planet. We proved they are human and of no threat to the American public. We cannot keep them locked up at the base forever. We cannot lock up innocent humans."

"Innocent humans? They're aliens, dammit!"

"THEY ARE NOT ALIENS!" Ted shouted at the general. It was his turn to be irate.

Not wanting to stoop down to the General's level of behavior, he took a breath to settle himself down. Regaining his composure, he continued. "They are clones of normal humans. The goo may have been alien, but the clones, the people, are *not* aliens."

Trying to diffuse some of the tension, Mr. Mason asked, "What about your escaped ali... er... resident? How do you know she won't do something else crazy? How do you know she won't attack once out in the general public?"

"They are no more likely to attack anyone than you or I. They want to learn and live... to live with the memory of a species that died a long time ago and a long way away."

"Ted, you can't do that. We can't allow it," Mr. Wright informed him.

"It's too late. I've already put the wheels in motion."

"WHAT?" the chairman bellowed.

"Yes."

The committee members loudly discussed the situation among themselves. Ted sat back in his chair. He knew he had done the right thing. He smiled as the committee tried to respond among the chaos. He quietly pulled out his cell phone and sent a text message to Carl.

committee in a panic :) green light

The committee members harrumphed among themselves for several more minutes, and then the general turned toward Ted. "This is intolerable! We cannot allow it!"

"As I told you, it's too late."

"Get them back!"

"I won't. And no one associated with this assignment will help. We're all prepared to lose our jobs. We will no longer keep these people locked up."

"Then we have no choice, Ted. We'll get them back ourselves." Turning to his committee colleagues, the Chairman instructed, "Get the Marines, call the Air Force, get the Secret Service... anyone. Get someone to that base and get those aliens back!"

The other men made phone calls and barked instructions.

Realizing they were serious, Ted quietly sent Carl another text message, hoping not to be noticed.

secret service alerted. go now. hurry.

Chapter 39 - Time to Go

The travelers assembled at the Exchange. The residents carried small duffle bags filled with their clothes and computers, plus the DVDs, and books they selected. TJ packed the video game consoles in boxes for the kids to have. The other counselors packed the DVD players in boxes for the adults to have. They also packed any remaining DVDs and books; even though they weren't selected by the residents. Mary, Denise, and Juliana packed boxes of clothes for those getting off at each destination. They thought nothing should go to waste. All of the boxes were stacked, waiting for the vans.

Carl received the second text message from Ted. "Okay folks, it's time to go. Let's not delay. Let's get moving." He was nervous. They had to move fast.

The travelers said goodbye to the counselors.

Two white vans pulled up. Carl rushed the travelers to get on board while the others loaded the boxes in the back. Carl took a count and realized they were one short. He couldn't hide his expression of panic. He looked toward the Exchange. Juliana came out carrying a box with the coffee maker hastily placed inside.

"Well... if we're taking the DVD players and video

games, why can't we take this?" she asked. "Martha and Patsy are gonna need it."

"Oh yes. We can't forget that," Carl replied sarcastically. "Now shall we go?" he said urgently.

Juliana put the box in the back, shut the rear doors and walked around to the side. She climbed in with the others and closed the door.

Carl got in the front seat of the second van. As they pulled away he rolled down the window and gave instructions to the counselors staying behind, "Leave now. Get off the base. Don't wait."

The vans drove to the airfield. Carl was obviously agitated. He motioned to the driver to go faster.

The vans stopped on the tarmac alongside the waiting jet and everyone got out. Carl instructed all to get on the plane. They climbed the steps and got on board the plane. Carl helped the drivers quickly load and secure the boxes on the plane. In the distance he heard the faint sound of sirens. He knew there was no city or town close to the base, so the sirens could only mean one thing. Carl thanked the drivers and motioned for them to leave quickly. He climbed the stairs and instructed the crew, "Okay gentlemen... let's get this door closed and get in the air quick."

"You got it sir," replied the co-pilot. "Let me get that door for you. Please take a seat and buckle up." The co-pilot folded the stairs, closed the door, returned to the cockpit and fastened his belt.

The jet engines revved and the plane started to move. With a couple turns they were on the runway and accelerating. Out his window Carl saw the black SUVs enter the airfield and drive toward the runway. "Get in the air!" he instructed the crew. "Don't stop. Mr. Stevens authorized this flight."

"Anything for my man Ted," the pilot responded through the open cockpit door. "Here we go."

The plane lifted off. As it banked and turned, Carl looked down at the ground. The Secret Service had reached the runway. The agents quickly got out and made calls on their cell phones as they looked at the vanishing plane.

Carl sat back in his seat, took a deep breath, and relaxed.

Chapter 40 - Trust the Data

Ted remained seated in his chair. He had not been dismissed by the committee.

After many minutes of discussing the situation while waiting to hear from the Secret Service agents, the committee members started to receive phone calls. More boisterous harrumphing ensued. The Chairman addressed Mr. Stevens. "TED! The plane took off before Secret Service could stop them!"

"Good."

"Dammit Ted! You're not cooperating! Where are they going?"

"East."

"Do you want to sacrifice your career for aliens?"

Calmly, Ted responded, "They are not aliens. They're people. Every bit of them, including their DNA is human. And yes, my team and I will sacrifice our careers for these people who do not deserve to be locked up. They have the right under our constitution to live free. They have the right to live their own lives the way they want. They are free U.S. citizens."

"The hell they are! We're going to find them. If you won't tell us where they are, we'll find them ourselves. We'll search high and low until we find them. Then we'll bring them back to the base. We'll lock them up and take over the containment operations."

"What are you going to do? Are you going to burst into these people's lives and just drag them away from their jobs and their neighbors?"

"Well... uh... yeah! That's just what we'll do! We're DHS, dammit!"

"What about all the witnesses? What about all the co-workers, neighbors, friends at the grocery store? Are you going to contain them too? How are you going to explain why you're putting innocent people into custody? And the children... how are you going to explain to teachers, friends, and neighbors why you're dragging away *children*?"

The committee members sat in silence for several moments. The chairman finally dropped his shoulders and sighed. He knew Ted was correct. He knew he could fight, but he wouldn't win. He gave up. "What are we supposed to do?"

"Trust me. Trust the data. You know they are human. They're innocent humans. Let them go. And leave them alone."

"How are we supposed to know these humans won't go alien on us, Ted? How do we know they'll live free and innocent?"

"Because they want to live free and innocent. They don't want to do anything else but live their own lives." He paused to let the committee member think. He continued, "I know where they'll be. My team and I will keep our eyes on them. We know how to stay in touch. And they want to stay in touch with us and each other. If something changes, we'll know about it. But since nothing will," Ted added, "we'll just let them live their lives."

The chairman forewarned Mr. Stevens, "I trust you also know how to stay touch with us."

Chapter 41 - Home

"It seems like ages ago since we were all put on a plane and sent to the base," Sue remembered. "But it wasn't that long ago."

"But yet, we've had a lot of time to meet each other," Donald added, "a lot of time to meet new friends and," he looked at Denise and Brandy, "new family."

"It seems weird that we're separating," Martha admitted. "I want to leave the base and live on my own, but I don't want to leave you guys."

"We'll still talk to each other," Sue assured everyone. "That's why they made phones!"

"Hey, Carl," Patsy jumped in, "why didn't we all get cell phones? We should have cell phones."

"Each of you has a regular phone at your residence."

"Yeah... but we want cell phones," Patsy responded. "What if I need to call Martha from work or from classes? What if Janet needs to call Larry? What if Sue needs to call Petunia to help with Kati and Violet?"

"Put them on your wish lists for Ted."

"Cool!" Patsy replied.

"So how will we know each other's telephone numbers?" Janet inquired. "How will we know how to talk to each other?"

"We have phone numbers for each of your houses," Carl answered. "We will give them to you when you get settled. Also, you'll be set up with internet access and email accounts."

"Good. I want to be able to talk to my friends," Janet replied.

"You'll make new friends in Wisconsin too, Janet," Mary told her.

"I know, but these people are my family. I want to stay close."

"Hey Carl," Sue called out, "will Ted let us visit each other? You know, fly to Wisconsin, or Arizona, or California?"

"I don't know," he answered honestly. "For now, I don't think so. But maybe after you all are well established. Put traveling on your wish lists also."

"Ted said that Janet and Larry would have to learn how to drive," Patsy recalled. "Why only them? Why won't Martha and I need to learn to drive? Why not Sue?"

"You'll be living near the campus of Arizona State University. You can walk most places and they have buses in the area if you need to travel a little further. You can get a bicycle and ride that too. Tempe is very bicycle-friendly."

"I guess I gotta put a bicycle on my wish list too," Patsy said.

"So do I," added Martha.

"You all are getting some expensive wish lists," Carl noted. "You know... at some point you will all have made enough money at your jobs to be able to buy whatever you need or want by yourselves. Eventually we won't pay for anything. You'll be on your own."

"But we can still talk to each other and talk to you and Mary, and Juliana and Denise, right?" Sue asked.

"Of course," Carl replied. "You'll just be on your own. You'll be independent. You'll be self-sufficient. You'll be taking care of yourselves. You'll be able to do almost anything you want."

"As long as we can still talk to each other, I'm good," Sue announced.

"Carl, who's going to teach us?" Zachary asked. "Will Sue?"

"You, Tyler, Kati, and Violet will go to school in Enterprise. Brandy will go to school in Burbank, California. You'll be in classrooms with other kids of your age."

"Are there other girls at school?" Violet wondered.

"Yes," Denise answered. "There will be many girls at school, Violet. You will meet lots of new friends at school."

"And don't forget Karen," Sue added. "She's six, like Kati. We'll be neighbors! She's really nice."

"Can I ride a bicycle to school?" Tyler inquired.

"I'm sure you can," Carl responded. "But you'll have to get a bicycle first."

"It's already on my wish list."

Shaking his head, Carl noted, "Ted's not going to like getting the bill for all the stuff on your wish lists."

"Is he paying with his money?" Donald asked Carl.

"No. That was a joke. The department is paying to move you and get you settled. Ted is in charge, but the government is paying."

"Good," Sue chimed in. "Ted has spent a lot of time taking care of us. He shouldn't have to pay for us."

The fasten seat belt indicator lit up and the tone pinged.

"That was fast," Denise observed. "We can't be in Arizona already... can we?"

Carl informed her, "In a private jet you can fly higher and faster than commercial. Makes it really nice to travel, doesn't it?"

"You're spoiled," Juliana told Carl. "I've only ever flown commercial. This is *way* nicer than I've ever flown."

"Okay everyone, please make sure your seat belt is fastened," Mary instructed.

"And your seat backs are in their upright position," Juliana added.

"And you tray tables are stowed," Denise finished.

Juliana and Denise laughed out loud. The others didn't. The others didn't know what was so funny, not ever having heard the instructions given on a commercial flight.

Feeling let down that only she and Juliana were laughing, Denise grumbled, "Man, you all really are spoiled."

The plane descended and landed. When it stopped on the tarmac, everyone got up out of their seats.

Carl called out instructions. "Okay, only Martha, Patsy, and Juliana are staying here in Phoenix. You can all get out to say goodbye, but the rest of you have to get back on the plane. Martha, Patsy, please remember to get your bags. We have two boxes of things for you as well."

"Three boxes," Juliana corrected him. "We have the coffee maker too."

"Right... can't forget the coffee maker. Okay, ready? Let's go."

The co-pilot opened the door for the passengers and unfolded the stairs. Everyone de-planed into the warm Arizona sun.

A black sedan pulled up. Only the driver got out. Sue and the others were expecting Ted to get out as well. They quickly forgot he was still back in Washington D.C., meeting with the department committee. The driver put the boxes and the duffle bags in the trunk. He stood and waited for his riders.

Talking loud over the noise of the idling jet engines, Juliana began saying goodbye. "Okay. This is where Martha and Patsy and I leave you. It's goodbye for now... but definitely not forever."

"We'll miss you," Sue told Juliana as she hugged her. "We need to call as soon as we can. And we'll visit soon, I hope."

Sue turned to Patsy and told her, "Study hard. Soon you'll be in college learning all kinds of smart things." She hugged Patsy. "Keep an eye on Martha and enjoy Arizona. We'll talk real soon... maybe even tonight."

Sue then hugged Martha and said, "I'll miss you most. We've been through a lot so far haven't we?" She and Martha looked at each other and smiled. "And there's a lot more to learn and do. Enjoy your new job. Now you can make coffee for lots of different people. And you'll meet lots of new people. You and Patsy will have fun together."

"You're my best friend, Sue," Martha responded. "I'll miss you too. But we'll talk and send messages every day. Have fun at your job. Cooking is what you love to do. You'll be great at it. And you'll be a great mother too. Kati and Violet are lucky to have someone like you to take care of them."

"Thanks Martha. We'll see you soon."

The others took their turns saying goodbye to the three women. Carl made sure Juliana understood all the instructions and information from Ted. He handed her a black portfolio. The driver opened the rear door for Martha and Patsy. Juliana climbed in the front seat. Everyone standing on the tarmac waved, but the windows were too dark to see if the women were waving back. The car drove off.

"Okay folks," Carl announced, "back on the plane. We have two more stops. Let's go."

Everyone climbed back into the plane and took seats. The co-pilot folded the stairs, closed the door, and took his seat next to the pilot in the cockpit. They all buckled up as the plane taxied to the runway.

Once in the air, the passengers moved about to have snacks and drinks. They had short conversations with each other, but nothing deep. A portion of their family had left. They knew it would happen. But now that they were gone, each felt the hole of the missing relatives. And they each knew the next stop would break them up further.

A little over an hour after take-off, the plane descended and landed.

"Okay, we're here in Abilene Kansas," Carl told Sue and the kids. "The van will drive you to Enterprise. Janet, you and Larry will get back on the plane with Mary and me, so you two do not need to bring your duffle bags. The rest of you... get your things."

The co-pilot opened the door and unfolded the stairs. They all deplaned into the crisp autumn air. They waited a few short moments for the van to arrive at the plane. The driver got out, opened the side doors for the passengers and helped Carl and the co-pilot transfer boxes and bags into the back.

Once again, Sue initiated the goodbyes. She hugged Janet. "We didn't have a lot of time to get to know each other. But I've enjoyed the time we've had. Stay in touch. Enjoy Wisconsin. Be good to Larry. Take care of him. We'll see you soon."

Janet smiled and nodded.

"We didn't have much time together, Larry, but I've enjoyed meeting you," Sue told him. "Good luck on your farm. Be good. Take care of Janet. She's good for you. We'll talk soon."

"I'll take care of Janet," he replied. "She and I will be good. I promise."

Sue hugged Mary and then Carl. "You have both helped us so much. We will not forget how many good things you have done for us. Thank you. Mary, enjoy Wisconsin. Carl, enjoy... wherever you end up. We'll stay in touch."

The others said goodbye and climbed into the van, leaving Janet, Larry, Mary, and Carl standing on the tarmac. The driver closed the side doors and gave Carl a little salute as he got in and drove away. The riders waved as the van departed, leaving the plane fading from view in the rear window.

After a short drive, the van arrived in Enterprise. When the van turned the corner and pulled into David's driveway, Sue saw a portable home in the backyard. In the front yard, David, Spike, Petunia, Susan, and Karen were waiting.

Sue told the others in the van, "I'm back at home."

The assembled people welcomed the travelers as they got

out of the van. "Sue!" Karen happily shouted.

Sue knelt down and told her little sister, "I'm called Suzanne now."

"Then welcome home, Suzanne," Karen replied.

"It's good to be home," Sue told her. Standing up and looking to each of the adults, she said, "Hello Susan, Spike, David, and Petunia."

David asked, "Can you introduce us to your friends, Suzanne?"

"Sure! First we have Kati, she's six. And Violet, she's seven. They are my daughters!"

Susan and Petunia were shocked. Karen smiled. She knew her big sister would be a good mother.

"And this is Tyler, he's eight," Sue continued. "And Zachary, he's twelve."

David announced to all, "They'll be living with me. I'll be their guardian."

"Guardian?" Sue questioned. "You'll be their father," she corrected.

"Yeah, I guess you're right," he responded, "I'll be their father." To Tyler and Zachary, David said, "Welcome to your new home, gentlemen."

"Thanks!" Tyler responded.

"Yeah, thanks!" Zachary added.

"And this is Donald," Sue continued. "He was a resident with us. This is his fiancée, Denise. She worked at the Exchange on the base. And this is their daughter, Brandy. She was a resident too. They're here with us for a few days and then they're going back to California to start their family."

"Hello all," David said to the visitors. He then made return introductions. "This is Susan Roberts. I'm sure you heard about her from Suzanne. This is Susan's daughter, Karen. I'm sure you heard about her, too."

"Once, maybe twice," Denise said sarcastically.

Sue smiled at Denise's comment.

This is Petunia Clark, Deputy Spike Leland, and I'm

David Hudson."

"Welcome to Enterprise, Kansas," Susan said to all.

"Shall we unload our boxes and bags?" Denise suggested.

"Sure. Let's bring them inside," David replied.

As David, Donald, and Denise moved the boxes and duffle bags into David's house, the kids clustered together and started getting to know Karen.

Sue pulled Susan aside to talk. "I hope you're okay with us living here," she told Susan.

"Well, to be honest... I wasn't at first. But Mr. Stevens visited a couple days ago. He told me the situation and convinced me that this was the best place for you. He said that you would be most comfortable here with 'your family', he called us. He suggested we could tell everyone we're cousins. That might explain why we look so similar. And I know you like Karen and she likes you a lot. She was very happy to hear you were coming back." Sue smiled. "Mr. Stevens said you'd be working at the Smokey Hill Café. You'll like it. And your new daughters will like it here. They'll go to school with Karen and play with her. They'll--"

"I hope *you* are okay with me living here," Sue told her, trying to confirm that Susan's life would not be completely disrupted.

"I am. I admit it's very weird," Susan said. "Mr. Stevens told me about the DNA testing and how we're the same."

"We're twins," Sue said. "More than twins, actually, we're exact copies. I can't think of another person I'd like to be a copy of."

"In a strange way, I think that's a compliment," Susan responded with a smile.

"It is."

"Thanks."

David stepped out the front door to talk to the two Sues. "Would you like to come inside? You can see where the boys will stay. Then we can take you to your house, Sue... er... Suzanne."

"We'd love to," Sue replied.

David led the parade of people on a tour of his house. He took special care to point things out to Tyler and Zachary. After the tour inside, they went out to the trailer in the back yard.

"Suzanne, this is where you, Kati, and Violet will be living until we get your new house built," David informed her.

"You mean this won't be our house?"

"No, it's only temporary until the permanent house, a bigger house, is built."

"We get a newer and bigger house than this?"

"Mr. Stevens arranged it," David told her.

"I have got to thank Ted the next time I see him. He's done so much for us. We wouldn't be here today if it wasn't for Ted."

Chapter 42 – You're Welcome

Four days after moving in, Sue returned from her first day at work. She was tired and smelled like grease from cooking all day. But the smell of grease was the smell of freedom. She rode a bicycle, Susan's bicycle, up David's driveway and into the garage. The kids had arrived home from school a few minutes earlier. They all ran up to Sue to say hello, each of them talking excitedly. They were all eager to tell her about their day at school and she was eager to tell them about her day at work. After hearing the commotion, David emerged from his house, followed by Donald, Denise, and Brandy. He suggested he get them all sodas while they take a seat on the patio out back.

As they all walked around the house, a green Toyota hybrid pulled in the driveway. A man in khaki pants and a Hawaiian print shirt got out. Thankfully for him, the air in Kansas had not yet turned frigid.

Sue, lagging behind the others, saw the man and called out, "Ted!" She ran over to him and gave him a big hug.

He gave Sue a big smile in return. "Hi Sue... er... I mean, Suzanne."

"Please, call me Sue."

"You're right. You'll always be Sue to me."

"Why are you here? Don't get me wrong, we're glad to see you, but why are you visiting?"

"I'm just checking in, you know, just saying hello."

"I want to thank you for everything, Ted. Not just for the job and the house and all that, but also for letting us live free. You have no idea how happy it's made us all. Thank you." She smiled at Ted.

"You're welcome," he replied, returning the smile.

"C'mon! The kids just got home from school. Join us out back."

Ted and Sue walked around the house to the backyard. As they rounded the corner, the kids saw Ted and ran over to him. "Uncle Ted!" they shouted in unison.

As they gathered around him, they said hello and told him about their days at school, their new houses, and their new city. Ted's smile became even wider.

Sue and Ted eventually took a seat at the table on the patio with the other adults. The kids ran to play in the back yard.

"Hello Ted. How are you?" Donald asked.

"Good, Donald. I'm good."

"So, what happened with the department?" Denise asked.

"Eh... not much. They yelled at me. I argued. I managed to escape unscathed."

"Do you still have a job?" she wondered.

"Of course," Ted quickly replied. "They can't scare me away. It takes a lot more than blustering to move me out of the picture."

"So what are you going to do?" Donald asked.

"Keep an eye on all of you, of course. And not take my job so seriously." He tugged at the bottom of his shirt and smiled. "How do you like my new wardrobe?"

"I like it," Denise replied.

"So do I," Sue added. "It makes you look younger."

Susan and Petunia entered the yard to visit their neighbors. They were warmly welcomed by all. Karen saw her mother and rushed over to tell her about her day. Then she zipped back to the yard just as fast to resume playing football with the other kids. The neighbors and friends jumped right into a conversation while seated around the patio table. They laughed and smiled as they talked.

Ted sat back and observed the kids and the adults all interacting with each other. He took a deep breath and smiled contently. He relaxed for the first time in a long time.

About the Author

Andrew D. Carlson is a biochemist and a writer. After receiving a degree from St. Olaf College, Andrew has worked in the biotech/pharmaceutical industry for over twenty years. He has embarked upon his second career as an author of fiction for young adults. *Sue's Fingerprint* is his debut novel. He has also written the sequels in the Sue trilogy: *Sue's Vision* and *Sue's Voice*. All are available at Amazon.com

Andrew lives in Los Angeles with his wife and son.

Follow Andrew:

On the web at http://andrewdcarlson.com

Twitter: @andrewdcarlson

Facebook Page: Sue's Fingerprint